Charnel House Blues:
The Vampyre's Tale

Charnel House Blues:
The Vampyre's Tale

Suzanne Ruthven

Winchester, UK
Washington, USA

First published by Sixth Books, 2014
Sixth Books is an imprint of John Hunt Publishing Ltd., Laurel House, Station Approach,
Alresford, Hants, SO24 9JH, UK
office1@jhpbooks.net
www.johnhuntpublishing.com
www.6th-books.com

For distributor details and how to order please visit the 'Ordering' section on our website.

ISBN: 978 1 78279 416 5

A CIP catalogue record for this book is available from the British Library.

Design: Lee Nash

Printed in the USA by Edwards Brothers Malloy

We operate a distinctive and ethical publishing philosophy in all
areas of our business, from our global network of authors to
production and worldwide distribution.

CONTENTS

Dedicated to the fond memory
of The Gothic Society
and its members: 1990–1998

"Through the whole vast shadowy world of ghosts and demons there is no figure so terrible, no figure so dreaded and abhorred, yet the cause of such fearful fascination as the vampire."
(Montague Summers, *The Vampire*)

"Much of Victorian death culture developed out of subconscious reactions to wide-spread death, new scientific discoveries and popular culture; these fears and anxieties were reflected in much of the Victorian era, which makes the time a perfect setting for a dark and creepy story."
(www.unhingedhistorian.blogspot.ie)

"Tolstoy, de Maupassant and Hoffman also wrote vampire stories. In fact the vampire stalks nineteenth century literature as persistently as he does twentieth century cinema ..."
(Patrick McGrath, *Bram Stoker & His Vampire*)

Prologue

It's a sorry fact, but vampires aren't what they used to be. I should know because I'm the last remaining member of my species from the *ancient* world; although if I'm brutally honest, this longevity is as much the product of becoming the *alter idem* of that club-footed Casanova, George Gordon, the sixth Lord Byron than any fortitude on my part. In truth, my roots are hinted at in that half-forgotten *Fragment* that was Byron's contribution to the Villa Diodati ghost story competition – for His Lordship *was* familiar with the decomposing vampire legends of the Eastern Mediterranean, even if John Polidori was not! But I get ahead of myself …

Today's vampires are a sorry lot. For 144 episodes, they allowed some chit of a girl to systematically vanquish anything and everything that smacked of vampirism, demons or any other forces of darkness in *Buffy: The Vampire Slayer*. The series catered for the young-adult market that tends to elevate action over subtly in the pursuit of its entertainment, and who still think that vampires are 'cool'. Well, we *are* to the touch, but I didn't think I'd ever live to see the day when the need to kill humans merely to exist would become *de rigueur* – for me it remains one of Life's bare necessities rather than actual pleasure. Nevertheless, I have always had a penchant for young ladies (preferably *over* high-school age) but the current glamorised trend for this kind of televised fiction makes the contemporary variety *so* susceptible to the vampire's 'kiss' – and, as the man said, 'the living is easy'.

At least *The Vampire Chronicles* harked back to the good old days of taste and refinement, but hell's teeth, Louis de Pointe du Lac was a feeble creature! His character had a permanent, petulant whine, with a persistently complaining note in it, which is about the most irritating trait any human voice can contain. The nightmare of being shut in close confinement with him

I

throughout the daylight hours of eternity would have been enough to cause any vampiric companion to impale him (or herself) on a boar spear and instantly perish. Mr Pitt (the actor not the politician) portrayed him admirably.

Lestat was cast more in the mould of a traditional vampire, but even he had some rather unsavoury and undiscerning habits that are, frankly, quite unpalatable to any self-respecting vampire. In short, Lestat de Lioncourt was a pervert in anybody's language, living or un-dead, who breached the realms of good taste and would kill anything with a pulse. And as for that infant Claudia – a petulant brat of a child, and even more so in her maturity – *that* idea was enough to set the alarm bells ringing in any premature burial, because who in their right mind would turn a five-year old child into a vampire without a thought for the consequences? I rest my case.

It must be evident that I am extremely well read when it comes to both classic and contemporary vampire fiction – after all there is very little to keep me amused in this world after rattling around the echoing vaults of eternity for so long. The film versions I watch on DVD, as the close proximity of so much sweating humanity I find unnerving in the close confines of a cinema. Some, I would truly class as 'horror films' due to their poor production or storylines rather than any horrifying elements in the script – after all, fact is often more horrifying than fiction.

So where, you may ask, are the other remnants of the Old World vampires who, according to tradition, cannot die? The majority of these poor creatures have perished because of their inability to adapt to contemporary living down through the ages. The old-fashioned bloodsuckers found themselves *a fronte praecipitium a tergo lupi,* which literally means 'a precipice in front, wolves behind', and unable to move forwards or back, they merely sat down and starved. A few of the more tenacious still lurk about on the periphery of Life but they are pitiful, desiccated creatures that exist on any sustenance they can draw from the rodents whose habitat they share.

For the true vampire's taste, blood should be savoured like fine wine, which means of course, that we do *not* go on a nightly rampage killing indiscriminately. The prey should be carefully selected and stalked with a hunter's eye – for who knows what trash that lithesome lovely may be using to pollute her body behind closed doors. An unspoiled Group A RH Positive should only be consumed once a month and savoured, whilst a weekly intake of an inferior drug or drink laced concoction would be the equivalent of binge-drinking courtesy of Oddbins! Snobbery perhaps, but there is undoubtedly a connection with the mystique of blood and the assumption of the superiority of one blood over another, but as the Romans would have observed: *de gustibus non est disputandum* – 'there's no accounting for tastes'.

I must also confess to a sneaking support for Jung and his 'collective unconscious' that harks back to certain primordial images for the basis of inducing uncontrollable and irrational fear into the mind of modern man. John Polidori, however, and to some extent that tiresome wench Caroline Lamb, unwittingly created a more 'modern' archetypal persona for the traditional vampire in the collective unconscious that superseded the 'race memory' version from folklore. If they hadn't written with such passionate *hatred* when creating their Lord Ruthven, the image of this deadly aristocrat would have remained securely within the realms of fiction and probably forgotten. Poor old George wasn't really half as bad as he was painted, but in his vampiric manifestation, he remains 'mad, bad and dangerous to know' – his reputation living on to fuel the fantasy of the un-dead in my own incarnation.

Polidori's 1819 novella, *The Vampyre*, originally introduced this concept of the charismatic, Byronesque anti-hero, but it was Bram Stoker's 1897 novel, *Dracula*, that is generally considered to be the quintessential vampire story, and which provided the basis (and the clichés) for most subsequent vampire fiction. Rather uncharitably, I thought, literary historian Susan Sellers maintained that the vampire has become "such a dominant figure in the horror genre that places the current vampire myth in the comparative safety of nightmare fantasy." In other words, familiarity diluted the element of fear and horror of the un-dead and rendered us relatively harmless! For all our harmlessness, however, the success of this 'nightmare fantasy' has spawned a distinctive new vampire genre with books, films, video games, and television shows ever on the increase. Unfortunately, the deadly erotic literary vampire that once could be viewed 'as adult as art gets' has degenerated into a mere teenagers' fantasy for role-players.

The concept of vampirism has existed for millennia and most cultures of the ancient world have their tales of blood-sucking demons. But despite the existence of such similar creatures, the entity you recognise today as 'the vampire' originates almost exclusively from Eastern Europe during the early 18th century, when the oral traditions of the many ethnic groups of the region were first being recorded and published by visiting folklorists, to later fuel the rapidly expanding literary – and then cinematic genres. Ironically, I find that I have now become a 'genre' which often causes me to smile.

And believe me, my friend, you have never fully lived until you've seen a vampire smile.

Chapter One

In Search of the Undead

Perhaps it would be a better introduction to the 'real' vampire if we went back in time to the ancient world from whence I came. There are some subtle differences between the Greek species of vampire, known as *'vrykolakas'* and the more well-known Slavic variety, which is written about at some length by John Cuthbert Lawson in a dusty old tome I discovered in Foyle's in the Charing Cross Road during one wet Wednesday afternoon. A scholar by nature, Lawson revealed that the 'secret' of the *vryko-lakas* can be found in the Greek tragedies of "corporeal return to avenge blood-guilt – a hidden theme due to the conventions of the Greek stage, but nevertheless clearly discernable" although the traditions of Greek drama only permitted a hint of such obligations.

> This bodily return was tacitly expected and feared in the case of blood-guilt and vengeance ... in ancient times murderers frequently mutilated their victims by cutting off their hands and feet and tucking them under the corpse's armpits, or binding them to its chest with a band. One rationale for this action that suggests itself is that such mutilation prevents the murdered victim from returning bodily to avenge itself on the murderer – who would, in turn, become a revenant wandering cursed between life and death ... the character of these Avengers approximates very closely to that of the modern *vrykolakes*. True, there is one fundamental difference; the ancient Avenger directed his wrath solely against the author of his sufferings ... the modern *vrykolakas* is unreasoning in his wrath and plagues indiscriminately all who fall in his way. Modern stories there are in plenty, which tell how the *vryko-*

lakas springs upon his victim and rends him and drinks his blood; how sheer terror of his aspect has driven men mad; how, in order to escape him, whole families have been driven forth from their native island to wander in exile; how death has often been the issue of his assaults; and how those whom a *vrykolakas* has slain become themselves *vrykolakes*.

You can imagine my delight at finding a serious book, published in 1910 and at the height of the *Dracula* craze that had a grasp of something other than peasant superstition! Poor old George obviously had knowledge of this background since his *Fragment* focuses on Smyrna rather than Transylvania, and he would be more inclined to the romanticism of Greece with its concept of honour killing than a marauding blood-sucker from the Balkans. This is not the place to go into my own personal history but suffice to say that I was called back to perform that obligation long before the advent of Christianity – which may go a long way to explain my sometimes archaic viewpoint. But let us return to the job in hand and give a true vampire's view of his fictional companions …

Perhaps we should start by attempting to view the 'cult of the vampire' objectively and dispassionately from a modern standpoint, and what better source to begin than with that thoroughly down-to-earth, 21ˢᵗ century online encyclopaedia, Wikipedia, for my introduction …

Vampires are mythological or folkloric beings who subsist by feeding on the life essence (generally in the form of blood) of living creatures, regardless of whether they are undead or a living person/being. Although vampiric entities have been recorded in many cultures, and may go back to 'prehistoric times', the term vampire was not popularised until the early 18th century, after an influx of vampire superstition into Western Europe from areas where vampire legends were frequent, such as the Balkans and Eastern Europe, although local variants were also known by different names, such as vrykolakas in Greece and strigoi in Romania.

Not strictly accurate my learned friend, since you obviously do not believe that such 'mythological' beings really exist, unlike the researches of two serious academics, Dr Raymond T McNally and native Romanian Professor Radu Florescu, who published *In Search of Dracula* (1973), chronicling their search for the 'real' Dracula and his castle. They, at least, were willing to give us the benefit of the doubt. As McNally muses:

> In Stoker's novel there were some fairly detailed descriptions of the towns ... and the Borgo Pass in the Carpathian mountains. These, too, proved real. If all that geographical data is genuine, I reasoned, why not Dracula himself? Most people, I suspect, have never asked this question, being generally thrown off by the vampire storyline. Obviously, since vampires do not exist, Dracula – so goes popular wisdom – must have been the product of a wild and wonderful imagination.

There is, of course, a universal saying that where there is smoke, there is always fire, and the enduring fascination with me and my kind continues to smoulder. The McNally-Florescu investigation discovered in authentic 15th-century manuscripts that confirmed there had been a "human being fully as horrifying as the vampire of fiction ... who had been the subject of many horror stories even during his own life time; a ruler whose cruelties were committed on such a massive scale that his evil reputation reached beyond the grave ..."

As a result, the team pieced together a dual history of the real 15th-century Dracula who came from Transylvania, and the vampires who existed in the legends of the same region. In addition, they reasoned that Bram Stoker in the 19th century combined these two separate traditions to create the most infamous vampire in all fiction – and raised several other questions. Was the real Dracula a vampire? Did the peasants of his time believe him to be a vampire? And was there any real connection between the historical tyrant and the character created by Stoker? Probably not, is the answer to all three but it is highly possible that Count Dracula's medieval thought-form was also given new life via Stoker's writing, just as my own ancient thought-form was re-animated by Bryon and Polidori.

Needless to say, these questions have now fallen by the wayside, since the popular currents of vampiric appreciation have whirled and eddied into realms that Count Dracula in particular, with all his schemes for world domination, could never have dreamed of while sleeping away the daylight hours in his Transylvanian tomb. For myself, on the other hand, there has never been *that* kind of ambition in my makeup.

It no longer matters whether the story of the charismatic vampire is fact or fantasy, the reading and film-going public acts as though we are real. But why, our critics demand to know, does this deadly creature continue to retain its icy stranglehold on popular imagination? Speaking from personal experience, despite the iciness of the vampire's 'kiss' it still incites a sense of erotic tension in intelligent women, and wistful envy in those males who are impressed by our power, both of whom remain captivated by this curious legacy.

The genuine vampire of Slavic folklore that eventually supplanted the Greek version was not a glamorous warrior-nobleman but a creature of plain peasant superstition. For example, there is a famous Serbian legend that tells of a certain Sava Savanović, who lived in a watermill and killed the millers so that it could drink their blood. The character was later used in a story written by Serbian writer Milovan Glišić, and in the Serbian 1973 horror film *Leptirica*, both of which were inspired by the tale.

But it wouldn't inspire a modern television production company to promote poor old Sava as the latest anti-hero for its latest generation of vampire lovers – after all who would look favourably on a simple, flour-dusted revenant straight from the Baker's Oven?

The modern vampire has metamorphosed from several different strands of folklore uniting as the different cultures came together. Raymond McNally and Radu Florescu, however, raised an important point in that according to Eastern Orthodox belief, the body of anyone bound by a curse will not be received by the earth – i.e. will not decay. The bodies of those who die under the ban of excommunication are doomed to remain 'incorrupt and entire' and that such beings ramble abroad at night, spending only the daylight hours in their tombs until absolution is granted. "All this goes a long way towards explaining why vampirism has been so credible in Orthodox countries," observed McNally – and why it is not applicable to one of a more ancient disposition!

Also, according to Orthodox Christian belief, the soul does not leave the body to enter the next world until 40 days after the body is laid in the grave, which also explains the ceremonies in Orthodox cemeteries 40 days after the burial. Bodies were once disinterred between three to seven years after burial and if the decomposition was not complete, a stake was driven through the heart of the corpse. On closer examination, it shows that the superstitions surrounding the causes of 'vampiric generation' are many and varied in original folklore and have only been in existence for a mere 600 hundred years in Eastern Europe.

There are so many superstitions surrounding vampires that have been repeated so often, it no longer surprises me that any genuine one could slip through the net. A dead person cannot become a vampire; they must be infected by another vampire while still living and even then, a victim will not become one of the 'undead' unless the biter wills it.

Who can become a vampire?

❖ **In Eastern Europe vampires are said to have two hearts, or two souls; since one heart or soul never dies, the vampire remains un-dead.**

Surely a tale invented by an insecure priesthood, since only the clergy are capable to creating such nonsense. I have one heart and my immortal soul is my own – and why do we never hear of *two* stakes being hammered into a vampire's hearts?

❖ **In Transylvania, criminals, bastards, witches, magician, excommunicants, those born with teeth or a caul, and unbaptised children. Also the seventh son of a seventh son is doomed to become a vampire.**

In other words anyone not the norm who the clergy deem to be beyond the pale and not accepted into the church; the seventh son of a seventh son is always known to be psychically gifted as a seer or healer, and the church wouldn't have liked the competition.

❖ **If a cat or other 'evil' animal jumps or flies over a dead body before it is buried, or if the shadow of a man falls upon the corpse, the deceased may become a vampire.**

This provided a good excuse for nailing down the coffin and getting on with the burial – probably to conceal any tell-tale signs of foul play and prevent any delay in collecting the inheritance.

❖ **If a dead body is reflected in a mirror, the reflection helps the spirit to leave the body and become a vampire.**

No doubt stemming from the belief that a vampire casts no reflection, but once clinically dead a person will not turn into a vampire no matter how bad their reputation.

❖ **A body with a wound that had not been treated with boiling water was also at risk.**

Gangrene poisoning produces the disgusting smell of

decaying flesh and would no doubt be associated with the grave in the minds of the peasantry.

❖ **In Russian folklore, vampires were said to have once been witches, or people who had rebelled against the Russian Orthodox Church while they were alive.**
Similar to the Transylvanian version of how to put the fear of God up the congregation, and provide a good excuse for a stake out.

How can a vampire be detected?

❖ **Any person who does not eat garlic, or who expresses a distinct aversion to garlic is suspect.**
And explains why most Eastern Europeans suffer from the most appalling halitosis, but if they don't reek of it they could become suspect and liable to be murdered.

❖ **Vampires sometimes strike people dumb. They can steal a person's beauty or strength; or milk from nursing mothers.**
I have often been struck dumb by the multitude of humans who are apparently eligible to become vampires – and we have no need of a mother's milk!

❖ **In Romania, peasants believe that the vampires and other spectres meet on St Andrew's Eve at a place where 'the cuckoo does not sing, and the dog does not bark'.**
Or where the sun does not shine!

❖ **One of the most common ways of locating a vampire was to choose a boy or girl young enough to be a virgin, and seat them on a horse of a solid colour – all white, brown or black – which was also a virgin and has never stumbled. The horse was then led through the cemetery and over all the graves. If it refused to pass over a grave, a vampire was thought to lie there.**
One can imagine the reaction if trying to perform *this*

particular rite in a municipal cemetery as a prelude to hauling corpses from the grave.

❖ **The tomb of a vampire usually has one or more holes roughly the size through which a serpent can pass.**
More likely for allowing decomposing gases to escape to prevent the tomb from exploding after consuming all that garlic.

How to create protection against a vampire?

❖ **Vampires are frightened by light, so one must build a good fire to ward them off, and torches must be lit and placed outside the houses.**
How on earth do they think we generated heat and light in our homes for centuries? Old world vampires may not cope with prolonged exposure to direct sunlight but we certainly enjoy the comfort of a roaring log fire, especially in Northern climates.

❖ **Even if you lock yourself up in your home, you are not safe from the vampire, since he can enter through chimneys and keyholes. Therefore, one must rub the chimney and keyholes with garlic, and the windows and doors as well. Farm animals must also be rubbed with garlic to protect them.**
Probably the most anti-social plant known to man after asafoetida. I know its protective uses go back to ancient Egypt but it is not surprising that so many Eastern Europeans migrated to England and America to get away from the stench.

❖ **Crosses made from the thorns of wild roses are effective in keeping the vampire away.**
The vicious thorns on a rose bush are a deterrent against anything; although I do know that the name 'dog rose' is said to have originated in Ancient Greece, where the root

was reputed to cure the bite from a rabid dog. A good example of cross-culture pollination, perhaps?

❖ **Spread thorns or poppy seeds on the paths leading to the village from the churchyard. Since the vampire must stop and pick up every one of them he may so be delayed that he cannot reach the village before sunrise, when he must return to his grave.**

Any vampire who falls for this stunt really should get out more!

❖ **Take a large black dog and paint an extra set of eyes on his forehead with white paint – this alienates vampires.**

Most large black dogs of my acquaintance would make friends with a vampire, and I have always had empathy with most members of the canine race – with or without painted faces.

❖ **Cultural practices often arose that were intended to prevent a recently deceased loved-one from turning into a vampire. Burying a corpse upside-down was widespread, as was placing earthly objects, such as scythes or sickle blades in the grave.**

This burial practice obviously brings to mind that vulgar music hall joke about where to park a bicycle, and would be more befitting a mother-in-law's burial than a loved one.

❖ **Other methods commonly practised in Europe included severing the tendons at the knees.**

This barbaric deterrent would only last as long as it took the vampire to regenerate himself – but it could buy the locals some valuable after-dark drinking time.

How to kill a vampire?

❖ **St George killed the dragon with a lance. One must impale the dragon, as one must impale the vampire.**

The only *guaranteed* method of killing a vampire – and possible the most dramatic from the filmmaker's point of view.

❖ **The stake must be driven through the vampire's body and into the earth in order to hold him securely in his grave. The stake should be made from a wild rose bush, or an ash, or asp tree. In some regions, red-hot iron rather than wood is used for the purpose. The vampire's body should be burned at the crossroads.**

Unless the stake pierces the heart it will not kill a vampire; burning the body is merely an added precaution – a sort of 'belt and braces' approach.

❖ **If the vampire is not found and rendered harmless, it first kills all members of its immediate family, then starts on the other inhabitants of the village and its animals.**

Probably a resultant folk tale following an outbreak of plague or typhus to explain why everyone in the locality is stricken; although it could be the original idea for *Salem's Lot*.

❖ **The vampire cannot stray far from his grave since he must return to it at sunrise.**

I can wander where I choose, although I prefer to avoid sunlight as this is extremely depleting, and have never returned to the grave since my original interment.

❖ **If not detected, the vampire climbs up into the belfry of the church and calls out the names of the villagers – who instantly die. Or, in some areas, the vampire rings the death-knell and all who hear it die on the spot.**

Only an idiot would draw attention to himself in such a manner and if he were 'undetected' it would be to his advantage to feed further away from home, not advertise his presence by ringing the dinner bell!

❖ **If the vampire is allowed to go undetected for seven years, he can travel to another country, or to a place where**

another language is spoken and become human again. He or she can marry and have children, but they all become vampires when they die.
I have travelled to many countries at will, speak several languages and, although not strictly a living human you would not be able to say there was anything different about my appearance. The latter I have not put to the test since I have no children to inherit my blood.

As you are no doubt aware, dear reader, tales of supernatural 'beings' consuming the blood (and sometimes the flesh) of the living have been found in nearly every culture around the world for many centuries. In modern parlance these beings would be identified as having vampiric tendencies, **but in ancient times, the term 'vampire' did not exist**; blood drinking and similar activities, including sexual perversions were attributed to night demons; even the Christian Devil (with whom I am *not* acquainted) was considered synonymous with vampirism. It was the Persians, I believe, who were one of the first civilizations to have tales of blood-drinking demons and in the 1970s novels, *Blood Summer* and *In Memory of Sarah Bailey* by Louise Cooper, the vampire legacy came from a demonic creature from this ancient world.

On my travels I have encountered many myths surrounding what must be referred to as my own kin, including those whose roots (like mine) are separate from the Balkan blood-suckers. The medieval chroniclers of 12th-century England, for example, Walter Map (who was actually Welsh) and William of Newburgh (*Historia rerum Anglicarum*) recorded accounts of 'revenants', although these appear to have quickly died out as far as English folklore is concerned. The Old Norse *draugr* is another medieval example of an un-dead creature with similar-ities to vampires. Fortunately for all of us, the cults and super-stitions that eventually passed into Northern European literature originated in this far older and widespread folklore and came to form the basis of the vampire legend that later spread to Germany and England, where it was subsequently embellished and popularised by the novels of Messrs Polidori, le Fanu and Stoker.

Nevertheless, the earliest recording of the lustiness of the 'undead' that shows you can't keep a good man down, came from the region of Istria in modern Croatia, in 1672. Villagers claimed that one Guire Grando had returned from the dead and had been drinking blood from his former neighbours and sexually harassing his widow. The village elder apparently soon put paid to Guire's nocturnal activities by ordering a stake to be driven through the corpse's heart, but when that didn't work, the locals cut off his head with more conclusive results. Although no one recorded what Madam Grando had to say on the subject of her deceased husband's amatory advances.

My newly discovered freedom enabled me to have my own bit of sport at the expense of those who would kill me if they had the opportunity, and I refer to those instances recorded by Paul Barber in *Vampires, Burial and Death: Folklore and Reality*, concerning the frenzy of vampire sightings in Eastern Europe during the 18th century. This resulted in frequent stakings and grave diggings to identify and destroy any potential revenants; even government officials engaged in the hunting and staking of vampires as their new 'blood sport'. "Despite being called the Age of Enlightenment," wrote Barber, "during which most folkloric legends were quelled, the belief in vampires increased dramatically, resulting in a mass hysteria throughout most of Europe. The panic began with an outbreak of alleged vampire attacks in East Prussia in 1721, and in the Habsburg Monarchy from 1725 to 1734, which spread to other localities."

The first two cases to be *officially* recorded, involved the corpses of Peter Plogojowitz and Arnold Paole from Serbia. These incidents were well documented by government officials who examined the bodies, wrote case reports, and published their results throughout Europe.

> The hysteria, commonly referred to as the '18th-Century Vampire Controversy', raged for a generation. The problem was exacerbated by rural epidemics of so-claimed vampire attacks, undoubtedly caused by the higher amount of superstition that was present in village communities, with locals digging up bodies and in some cases, staking them. Although many scholars reported during this period that vampires did not exist, and attributed reports to premature burial or rabies, superstitious belief increased.

Although my involvement went undetected, it gave me a new lease of life, so to speak. French theologian and scholar, Dom Augustine Calmet compiled a rather ambiguous treatise (1746) amassing reports of incidents, which many serious minded people (including a critical Voltaire and supportive demonologists) interpreted as claiming that vampires *did* exist. In his *Philosophical Dictionary*, Voltaire wrote:

> These vampires were corpses, who went out of their graves at night to suck the blood of the living, either at their throats or stomachs, after which they returned to their cemeteries. The persons so sucked waned, grew pale, and fell into consumption; while the sucking corpses grew fat, got rosy, and enjoyed an excellent appetite. It was in Poland, Hungary, Silesia, Moravia, Austria, and Lorraine, that the dead made this good cheer.

The 'Vampire Controversy' that I instigated single-handedly only ceased due to the onset of boredom on my part, and the intervention of the Empress Maria Theresa of Austria, who sent her personal physician to investigate the claims of these vampiric entities. The conclusion was that vampires did *not* exist and the laws prohibiting the opening of graves and desecration of bodies were passed, which effectively put paid to the vampire hysteria. Despite this imperial condemnation, by giving it 'international coverage' by the Reuters equivalent of the day, the entire vampire-cult had been given yet another new lease of life – to live on in literature, folklore and cinema.

Europe has never been backward in producing its own fair share of monsters among the living. As the McNally-Florescu investigation revealed in *In Search of Dracula,* a certain 'Count Dracula' was in fact an authentic 15th-century Wallachian prince who was often described in contemporary manuscripts and popular horror stories as "an awesome, cruel, and possibly demented ruler." He was known mostly for the amount of blood he indiscriminately spilled, not only of the infidel Turks – which, by the lights of his time, would have made him a hero – but also that of his neighbours. "His ingenious mind devised all kinds of tortures, both physical and mental, and his favourite way of imposing death has caused Romanian historians to label him 'Vlad the Impaler'," although the researches shy away from raising the question of his mental condition, which was extreme even for the times in which he lived.

By way of a compromise, however, McNally-Florescu reasoned that in a rogue's gallery he would have competed for first prize with Cesare Borgia, Catherine de Medicis or Jack the Ripper, owing not only to quantity of his victims, but to the refinements of his cruelty. They also considered the names of Dracula and his father Dracul as being of great importance, since both having the given name 'Vlad', the names 'Dracul' and 'Dracula' were really nicknames with a dual meaning. Dracul meant 'devil' and also 'dragon' with Vlad senior being invested by the Holy Roman Emperor Sigismund, with the Order of the Dragon, a semi-monastic, semi-military organisation dedicated to fighting the Turks.

As for the son, we now know that he had two nicknames: he was called Vlad Tepes, which signifies 'Vlad the Impaler', and he was called Dracula, a diminutive meaning 'son of the dragon' or 'son of the devil'. A final point in this discussion of nomenclature: the interchangeability of the words 'devil' and 'vampire' in many languages may be one reason for the association of Dracula with vampirism ... In an age of violence all the Draculas lived violently and, with few exceptions, died violently.

In my own defence I have to state that apart from during the 'Vampire Controversy' I have never killed for pleasure. After hundreds of years of close confinement, my release brought about a kind of hysteria that needed to let off steam in a manner that had an entire government chasing its tale. The intervention of the Empress was what saved them as I would never be so insensitive as to disoblige a lady – even if she denied my existence.

Peasant superstition, however, is extremely tenuous and in *Transylvanian Superstitions* dating from as late as 1885, Madame Emily de Laszowska Gerard confirmed that every Roumenian [*sic*] peasant *still* believed in vampires (or *nosferatu*) as "firmly as he does in heaven or hell." According to the author, there were two sorts of vampire – living and dead. The living are generally the illegitimate off-spring of two illegitimate people, "but even a flawless pedigree will not ensure anyone against the intrusion of a vampire into his family vault, since every person killed by a *nosferatu* becomes likewise a vampire after death, and will continue to suck the blood of other innocent people till the spirit has been exorcised, either by opening the grave of the person suspected and driving a stake though the corpse, or firing a pistol shot into the coffin." In very obstinate cases it was further recommended to cut off the head and replace it in the coffin with the mouth filled with garlic, or to extract the heart and burn it, strewing the ashes over the grave. "That such remedies are often resorted to," she continued, "even in our enlightened days, is a well-attested fact, and there are probably few Roumenian villages where such has not taken place within the memory of the inhabitants."

The 17th and 18th centuries, however, were intellectually turbulent times in Europe, and although being known as the Age of Enlightenment (or the Age of Reason) there remained a peculiar juxtaposition of cultural peculiarities. Reason challenged ideas grounded in faith, tradition and superstition, but it was nevertheless a time when these elements were demonstrated to still be firmly entrenched in the art of the period. Subsequently, Reason eventually surrendered to Romanticism – an artistic, literary, and intellectual movement that originated in Europe toward the end of the 18th century – when everything was viewed through rose-tinted spectacles and fragranced with an incense of attar of roses: even mad princes and vampires.

"The word [Romanticism] derives from the late-eighteen-century vogue for medieval tales of adventure (such as the legends of King Arthur or the Holy Grail, called "romances" because they were written in a Romance language, not in Latin). But this interest in the long-neglected "Gothick" past was symptomatic of a general revulsion against the established social order and established religion – against established values of any sort – that sprang from a craving for emotional experience. Almost any experience would do, real or imaginary, provided it was sufficiently intense."
The History of Art – H W Janson

Stephen Little in *...isms: Understanding Art*, also blew the incense smoke in the eyes of his readers by explaining that Romanticism was a very broad movement that "valued human emotions, instincts and intuitions over rationality and surprisingly, horror and the supernatural also played a role in Romanticism, partly as a result of the suffering caused by the Napoleonic Wars, partly because of the significance accorded to private worlds of myth and fantasy."

In addition to all this idealised thinking, The Grand Tour allowed young men of privilege to tour the Continent, or as Matt Gross of the *New York Times* described it:

> Three hundred years ago, wealthy young Englishmen began taking a post-Oxbridge trek through France and Italy in search of art, culture and the roots of Western civilization. With nearly unlimited funds, aristocratic connections and months (or years) to roam, they commissioned paintings, perfected their language skills and mingled with the upper crust of the Continent …

Along with all these treasures, they would also have brought home the tall tales they had heard along the way of ghostly and supernatural doings, and others would subsequently write about them. And it was during the 18th century that I really came into my own …

The literary vampire (myself included) having its roots in Romanticism, actually evolved out of that famous collection of ghost stories – *Fantasmagoriana* – from the Villa Diadoti, that inspired the creators of the modern genre. Not surprisingly, the erotic undercurrents prevalent among the company at the Villa would have strongly influenced Polidori's writing, coupled with the fictional hatchet job wielded by Caroline Lamb after Byron had left England. Everyone is familiar with the story as told by Percy Shelley in the Preface to the first edition of his sister's *Frankenstein*:

> The season was cold and rainy, and in the evenings we crowded around a blazing wood fire, and occasionally

amused ourselves with some German stories of ghosts, which happened to fall into our hands. These tales excited in us a playful desire of imitation. Two other friends ... and myself agreed to write a story, founded on some supernatural occurrence ...

I have since discovered that these German 'shudder' stories had a tremendous influence on the development of the English Gothic literary genre and according to Dr Hale of the Performance Translation Centre at the University of Hull, "frequently employed traditional folk-motifs coupled with increasingly sophisticated narrative techniques." A technique that is often still highly identifiable in the literary genre of the 20th century. Until the Romantics came along, however, the vampire was still a creature to inspire fear and revulsion rather than emanating the 'compulsive eroticism' of the literati-inspired anti-heroes of Polidori, Le Fanu and Stoker.

Ironically, although most cultures do have their blood-sucking demons, and the traditional vampire folklore phenomena were generally restricted to Eastern Europe, the most famous vampires of all were actual creations of English and Irish writers. Since there was no home-grown folklore to provide background details for the stories the authors were forced to research native sources; although the French had localised traditions of werewolves, which they eventually took with them to the New World. Nevertheless, the town of Whitby in North Yorkshire with its ruined Benedictine abbey continues to inspire pilgrimages for *Dracula* fans from across the world, while the abbey ruins on the North Cliff overlooking the North Sea, remain a prominent landmark for sailors where the *Demeter* came ashore ...

Chapter Two

The Vampyre

By the late 17th century I had degenerated into a mere 'thought-form', something that exists on the periphery of the imagination or memory, inhabiting that dismal mudbank, surrounded by a circle of stagnant pools where, 100 years later poor old George Byron was to meet his end. I survived by leeching off the most unappetising of creatures but *fames optimum condimentum* as they say – hunger is the best seasoning. News came to me on the breeze of the stirrings in East Prussia in 1721 and I painfully made my way from Greece to seek news of my kin.

The rumours, however, were false. The vampire sightings from what I can gather were cases of premature burial and the superstitious reaction to those poor souls who had been interred in the grave while yet living. Nevertheless, the journey cured me of my ennui and during the next few years I applied myself to the most intense programme of learning the Age of Enlightenment had to offer. Besides, there were new delights to sample in the company of those young men who were making the Grand Tour and seeking new experiences away from the watchful eyes of their peers. Travelling through Italy and France I discovered that there was no vice they would decline to partic-ipate in, in order to further their education. With their unlimited funding and the right connections, I was able to improve *my* language skills and be received by some of the most influential families in Europe in exchange for my introduction to the darker side of Life.

In the intervening years I was again passing through that dreadful place at Missolonghi when by chance I met Lord Byron in the winter of 1809. He was eager to see the home of the Muses, and to drink from the Castalian Spring, so we crossed the Gulf of

Corinth together and rode up the valley to Castri, the site of ancient Delphi, on the slopes of Parnassus. During this journey I told him many tales from my homeland for his amusement but little did I think that I was sowing the grains for my own immortality. Did he remember me when penning *A Fragment* ... I believe he did.

Many years later the literary-metamorphosed vampire that emerged from the Villa Diadoti 'ghost story' contest quickly developed a life force of its own – which was not surprising since it was the collective brainchild of Byron and his physician John Polidori – and created a minor literary scandal when it was published in 1818. *The Vampyre* was based on Lord Byron's unfinished story *Fragment of a Novel*, published in 1819, but it is arguably the most influential vampire work of the early 19th century, inspiring such works as *Varney the Vampire, Carmilla* and eventually *Dracula*.

As the literary editor of *The Vampyre & Other Stories* observes, *The Vampyre* is "quite different in mode and construction from *A Fragment*, but it is possible to see where some of the facets of Polidori's own tale came from and why he later insisted so vehemently on the groundwork of *The Vampyre* being Lord Byron's ..." There is no suggestion in Byron's fragment that his anti-hero Darvell was a vampire, but Polidori later declared that this was so "and Byron himself is supposed to have referred to his fragment as 'My real *Vampyre*'." I alone recognise the elements of those tales related to his Lordship during that trip to Delphi that must have lain dormant in his mind in those intervening years, and which he must have retold to Polidori during their travels.

Polidori's aristocratic vampire with "... the deadly hue of his face, which never gained a warmer tint, though its form and outline were beautiful ..." set the tone for all future vampiric anti-heroes (with the exception of the unfortunate *Nosferatu*), and it was said that the author had spitefully cast Bryon himself as the charismatic but deadly 'Lord Ruthven'. A name already made notorious by Lady Caroline Lamb, who had used it for her own portrait of Byron in her Gothic novel, *Glenarvon*, complete with ghosts, ruins, and rumours of strange rites that involve the drinking of human blood, published just weeks after Byron's departure from England (1816). That this was common knowledge is reflected in J C Hobhouse's (Byron's friend, Lord Broughton) record: "Yesterday Lady Caroline Lamb published a novel, *Glenarvon*. The hero is a monster, and meant for Byron." Her second novel, *Ada Reis*, also represented Byron as 'the evil one' but it couldn't match *Glenarvon* for sheer malice ...

That which was disgusting or terrific to man's nature had no power over Glenarvon. He had looked upon the dying and the dead, had seen the tear of agony without emotion; had heard the shriek of despair, and felt the hot blood as it flowed from the heart of a murdered enemy, not turned from the sickening sight ...

Lord Byron, Joanna Richardson

These attributes were also maliciously reflected in Polidori's young hero's observations that Lord Ruthven's "irresistible powers of seduction" always resulted in his victim being "hurled from the pinnacle of unsullied virtue, down to the lowest abyss of infamy and degradation" ...

There was one circumstance about the charity of his Lordship ... all those upon whom it was bestowed, inevitably found that there was a curse upon it, for they all were either led to the scaffold, or sunk to the lowest and the most abject misery ... If it had before entered into his imagination that there was an evil power resident in his companion these [letters] seemed to give him almost sufficient reason for belief. His guardians insisted upon him immediately leaving his friend, and urged, that his character was dreadfully vicious, for that the possession of irresistible powers of seduction, rendered his licentious habits more dangerous to society.

These characteristics became synonymous with the Gothic genre and the vampire culture in general, being both alluring and sexual, but remaining linked with horror and supernatural terror. Apart from Lord Ruthven's sinister aura, deceptive physical strength and mesmerising influence, he was able to move freely in society at all times, in pursuit of his virgin prey. The theme was instantly popular and several other authors quickly adapted the character of Lord Ruthven into other works. Cyprien Bérard wrote an 1820 novel, *Lord Ruthwen ou les Vampires*, which was at the time falsely attributed to Charles Nodier. Nodier himself wrote an 1820 play, *Le Vampire*, which was adapted back into English for the London stage by James Robinson Planche as *The Vampire*, or *The Bride of the Isles*. At least four other stage versions of the story also appeared in 1820.

In 1828, Marschner and Wohlbrück adapted the story into a German opera, *Der Vampyr*. A second German opera with the same title was written in 1828 by Lindpaintner and Heigel, but the vampire in Lindpaintner's opera was named Aubri, not Ruthven. Dion Boucicault revived the character in his 1852 play *The Vampire: A Phantasm*, and played the title role during its long run. Alexandre Dumas (père) also used the character in an 1852 play – *Le Vampire*; while in *The Count of Monte Cristo*, the principal character Edmond Dantès is often referred to as 'Lord Ruthven' by Countess G, who incorrectly attributes the creation of Ruthven to Lord Byron.

A Lord Ruthven also appeared in the Swedish novel *Vampyren* (1848), the first published work by author and poet Viktor Rydberg; as the story unfolds, it becomes clear that he is inspired by him in name only: *this* Ruthven is actually no supernatural being at all, but a deranged psychopath *believing* himself to be a vampire.

As contemporary Gothic author and artist Franklin Bishop observes, however, John Polidori "was responsible for introducing into English fiction the enduring image of the vampyre in the guise of a suave, cynical and murderous English Lord. With the presentation of Lord Ruthven [Byron] as a vampyre, Polidori created a personification of evil that countless authors have since imitated in attempting to satisfy the enormous public interest in this genre of literature." Nevertheless, it was not until poor old George's death at Missolonghi on Easter Monday, 19th April 1824 that my metamorphosis was complete and I became his *alter idem*, his 'other self' that will endure as long as Byron's name and his works are in the public domain.

Nevertheless, after the appearance of *Dracula* in 1897, the Count took over as the stereotype for the aristocratic vampire, although according to the entry in Wikipedia, Lord Ruthven has since had many manifestations in various forms – films, comic book format (including *Superman* and *Marvel* comics), computer games, and an alternative history (the *Anno Dracula* series) amongst others. I can't say that I'm impressed with my name being used in this way but it is a means of keeping the identity alive, and the means by which the thought-form remains flesh.

Nearly 30 years later, Thomas Preskett Prest, published *Varney the Vampire*, or *The Feast of Blood*, as the first instalment of a 'penny dreadful' in 1847, which was reprinted in 1853. Before writing it, the author had studied the vampire legends in detail but oddly enough for the time, Sir Francis Varney was cast as a basically good person who has been driven to evil by personal circumstances. He often tries to redeem himself but at the end of the novel, despair drives him to commit suicide by jumping into the crater of Mount Vesuvius!

The figure turns half round, and the light falls upon the face. It is perfectly white – perfectly bloodless. The eyes look like polished tin; the lips drawn back and the principal feature next to those dreadful eyes is the teeth – the fearful looking teeth – projecting like those of some wild animal, hideously, glaringly white and fanglike … It clashes together the long nails that literally appear to hang from the finger ends …

The novel itself is tediously long and repetitive – and lacks continuity in the plot due to it being originally written in instalments and often by different people. For example, Sir Francis Varney reappears with dark and lustrous eyes, a pleasant voice and a 'bland almost beautiful smile', rather than the creature of nightmare that manifested in the first chapter – although no explanation is given for this transformation. Perhaps Prest realised his mistake in making his vampire too ghoulish if he wanted his female characters to fall under his spell; or was using the traditional device of having his vampire able to voluntarily alter his appearance – but failing to mention it in the narrative.

Nevertheless, *Varney* was another major influence on later vampire fiction and, according to cultural historian David Skal in *V Is for Vampire: The A to Z Guide to Everything Undead*:

Many of today's standard vampire tropes originated in *Varney*: Varney has fangs, leaves two puncture wounds on the necks of his victims, has hypnotic powers, and has superhuman strength. Unlike later fictional vampires, he is able to go about in daylight and has no particular fear of either crosses or garlic. He can eat and drink in human fashion as a form of disguise, but he points out that human food and drink do not agree with him. His vampirism seems to be a fit that comes on him when his vital energy begins to run low; he is a regular, normally functioning person between feedings.

As near to the truth as this account may be, it is probably safe to say, however, that neither myself nor Count Dracula would have ever contemplated such a voluntary and ignominious end: Polidori's and Stoker's vampires were made of sterner stuff.

If I were seeking a vampiress of unparallel virtue, I would look no further than an

Irish author with the unlikely name of Joseph Sheridan Le Fanu, who was the next to fall under the spell. He wrote the novella *Carmilla* (1872) for *In A Glass Darkly* – said to be possibly one of the greatest vampire stories of all time – but this time creating the most famous female vampire in the genre. Le Fanu's description of how a person becomes a vampire is based upon authentic folk-belief from Eastern Europe, and in this novella Bram Stoker found the basic ingredients to encourage him to delve seriously into vampire mythology for his own literary inspiration.

Carmilla was, of course, beautiful and captivating. In the Introduction to the 1995 Wordsworth reprint of *In A Glass Darkly*, it states, "This story is a curious mixture of traditional vampire-lore and Irish folklore. The beautiful vampire Carmilla has much in common with traditional Irish female spirits who were often attached to a particular family, though her strong sexuality is a characteristic vampire attribute." The description of this exquisite creature is given from Laura, Carmilla's intended victim's perspective:

> She was slender, and wonderfully graceful. Except that her movements were languid … Her complexion was rich and brilliant; her features were small and beautifully formed; her eyes large, dark and lustrous; her hair was wonderful, I never saw hair so magnificently thick and long when it was down about her shoulders … It was exquisitely fine and soft, and in colour a rich very dark brown, with something of gold …

Despite suggestions in later writings on the subject, there appears to be no real evidence to suggest that Le Fanu based

Carmilla on the notorious real-life 'Countess Dracula' – in reality Elizabeth Bathory – although the names are frequently linked on the grounds that both characters were female and Le Fanu *may* have heard something of her history. *Carmilla*, I'm glad to say, lacks the calculating, sadistic cruelty of the original 'Blood Countess' and Le Fanu assiduously avoids any suggestion of this in his character. When Bram Stoker introduced his anti-hero to the reading public, few would have known he could also have been influenced by an authentic historical character.

Avoiding the Byronic handsomeness, Stoker describes Dracula as a "tall old man, clean-shaven save for a long white moustache and clad in black from head to foot without a single speck of colour around him anywhere." The author depicts Dracula's moustache as heavy, his teeth as sharp and white, and his skin as sallow and pallid. In the existing portrait of Dracula that survives in the collection at Castle Ambras, the *real* Dracula is as startling and arresting in appearance as the figure created in words by Stoker, unlike the cadaveristic – and rather revolting – creature, Nosferatu, created some years later by Max Schreck in Murnau's classic horror film of the same name. Stoker's description continues ...

> His face was a strong – a very strong – aquiline, with high bridge of the thin nose and peculiarly arched nostrils; with lofty domed forehead, and hair growing scantily around the temples, but profusely elsewhere. His eyebrows were very massive, almost meeting over the nose, and with bushy hair that seemed to curl in its own profusion. The mouth ... was fixed and rather cruel-looking, with peculiarly sharp white teeth; these protruded over the lips, whose remarkable ruddiness showed astonishing vitality in a man of his years. For the rest, his ears were pale and at the tops extremely pointed; the chin was broad and strong ...

It was fascinating to read 'The Curse of the Unread' (*The Goth* v.9 1992), in which Tina Rath makes a rather thought provoking revelation. "The description," she writes, "is particularly interesting because it is so different from the current conventional image of the Count. The cinematic versions which have made such a deep impression on the popular picture of the vampire include the rodent fangs of Klaus Kinski's remake of *Nosferatu*, Christopher Lee's remarkable height and red contact lenses in the Hammer *Draculas*, Lugosi's smooth middle-European gigolo, and Langella's consciously Byronic image, tousle hair and shirt open *à là victime* in the 1931 and 1979 versions of *Dracula* respectively – but nowhere amongst these diverse images do we find an old man with a long white moustache."

Tina Rath also points out that Stoker himself altered Dracula's image for his reappearance in London, wearing a "pointed beard with a few white hairs running thought it." But why do we have all these conflicting images of a single character? Rath's suggestion is because, surprisingly enough, *Dracula* is probably one of the best-known, but **least-read** books in the horror genre; and filmmakers of the time were notorious for casting an attractive leading man and re-writing the script accordingly. Nevertheless, we know that Dracula is a 'shape shifter' and so he may have appeared to Harker as an old man, in order to allay any fears the younger man may have had; and to his victims Stoker may have intended to portray the Count with a more attractive image. The mystery is solved when Harker discovers the Count's body in the makeshift wooden coffin on the evening prior to his departure for England "…looking as if his youth had been half-renewed … for on the lips were gouts of fresh blood …"

Since I have also explored many of the occult sciences and become quite proficient in their application, it was no surprise that Dracula is a shape shifter, often appearing in the form of mist or phosphorescent specks; the Romanian vampire of folklore also sometimes comes as points of lights shimmering in the air. Stoker's vampire can also turn into a wolf or a bat, particularly the latter; and Transylvania folklore links the bat with vampirism. He also comes ashore at Whitby in the form of an immense dog. Following Slavic folklore, Stoker's vampire moves only at night, casts no reflection in a mirror, and is repelled by the sign of the cross.

The latter are demonstrated on the second morning of Harker's visit to the castle when the Count enters his room and casts no form in the shaving mirror. The surprise causes Harker to nick his chin with the razor causing the Count's eyes to "blaze with a sort of demoniac fury", and he suddenly made a lunge at his visitor's throat. His fingers touch the string of beads holding the crucifix given to Harker by a peasant woman on his leaving the last inn on his journey, and instantly recoils ... and Harker discovers that he is a "veritable prisoner" within the castle. His feelings of terror and revulsion are not lessened by the night-vision of the Count crawling headfirst down the precipitous walls of the castle, "with his cloak spreading out around him like great wings."

Fiction and folklore make a great deal of the preventative methods for keeping revenants at bay but in all honesty, few are effective against the strength of the vampire's will. An apotropaic, is an amulet worn to ward off an attack, and occurs in all vampire folklore – garlic being the most common in literature, although the rarely used wood from the wild rose and hawthorn is believed to have the same affect. Other amulets include any sacred items such as a crucifix, rosary, bible or holy water – unless your vampire happens to be Jewish as in the case of Roman Polanski's film *Dance of the Vampires* (1967: called *The Fearless Vampire Killers* in the USA), or of ancient Greek lineage like myself!

The Balkan bloodsuckers, however, are said to be unable to walk on consecrated ground, such as that of churches or temples, or cross running water, although the Count expresses his delight that Carfax has "a chapel of old times" and there are often vampire encounters in cemeteries novels. Some vampires have no reflection in a mirror or cast no shadow but this by no means universal; similarly some traditions belief that a vampire cannot enter a house uninvited – although after the first invitation they can come and go as they please. Though folkloric vampires were believed to be more active at night, they were not necessarily vulnerable to sunlight, and all these contradictions made it possible for later writers of vampire fiction to make it up as they went along. I often look at myself in the mirror, not through vanity but marvelling at the likeness between myself and that long-dead poet who bore only a fleeting resemblance to my earlier Greek self.

When Val Helsing and his merry band hold their council of war prior to going off in search of Dracula, the Professor reports what he's learned from his old chum at Buda-Pest University about their adversary. It appears that the fiend they are up against is Voivode [sic] Dracula, who had certain occult powers fuelled by his "mighty brain and iron resolution." Listing his magical abilities, Van Helsing claims they are up against one who has the strength of twenty men … cunning that has the growth of ages … the aids of necromancy … and power over the dead. "He can, within limitations, appear at will when, and where, and in any of the forms that are available to him; he can within his range, direct the elements: the storm, the fog, the thunder; he can command all the meaner things: the rat, and the owl, and the bat – the moth, and the fox, and the wolf; he can grow and become small; and he can at times vanish and come unknown." All of which makes the Count a rather a formidable customer to deal with when it comes to killing him, since he appears to have the powers of Merlin and Superman combined! If only I could have accomplished half …

Despite the methods of repelling a vampire being relatively

simple, the actual methods of destruction are numerous, complicated and extremely time-consuming. The most frequently cited is to drive a wooden stake through the heart, usually ash, rose or hawthorn, or sometimes oak, depending on the location and according to local tradition. There were, of course, variations using metal implements instead of wood – which were interred with the corpse at the time of burial. A vampire could also be killed by being shot (silver bullet optional); by being drowned in running water; or the sprinkling of holy water on the body. The latter I can assure you is completely ineffective, and *no* living creature will survive being staked through the heart, never mind a vampire.

But to continue … decapitation featured strongly when disposing of vampires, with the head buried between the feet, behind the buttocks, or away from the body. In some cases the body was dismembered, the pieces burned and the ashes scattered into fast flowing water. Van Helsing cut off the lovely Lucy's head and stuffed the mouth with garlic. Another common way of destroying vampires was by fire – hence European witches being burned at the stake to prevent them from becoming vampires, according to Montague Summers (who is not always a reliable source for these matters). Alternatives to a stake through the heart was the use of a consecrated dagger (which was used to despatch Dracula), or a silver bullet. A vampire should only be struck once or it will reanimate; and care should be taken not to expose a vampire's body to moonlight, as this will also restore it to 'life'. Surprisingly, the latter was ignored by Stoker in his novel, while Sir Francis Varney was restored by this method having been shot by Flora Bannerworth. Poor Carmilla, however, was dealt with in the traditional manner:

> The grave of the Countess Mircalla was opened … The features, though a hundred and fifty years had passed since her funeral, were tinted with the warmth of life. Her eyes were

open; no cadaverous smell exhaled from the coffin ... there was a faint but appreciable respiration, and a corresponding action of the heart. The limbs were perfectly flexible, the flesh elastic; and the leaden coffin floated with blood, in which to the depth of seven inches, the body lay immersed. Here then, were all the admitted signs and proofs of vampirism. The body, therefore in accordance with the ancient practice, was raised, and a sharp stake driven through the heart of the vampire, who uttered a piercing shriek ... the head was struck off, and a torrent of blood flowed from the severed neck. The body and head were next placed on a pile of wood, and reduced to ashes, which were thrown upon the river and borne away ...

With all his occult powers, I wonder if there are those who, like myself, are dissatisfied with the ease and manner of the Count's death. Dracula was overtaken on his dash back to his tomb at Castle Dracula and ignominiously despatched when his wooden crate fell from the wagon and burst open on the road. Stoker's description provides rather a pitiful anti-climax after such a melodramatic chain of events, and leaves the reader with the impression that the author ran out of ideas at the end of the novel. An adversary of that calibre shouldn't have been despatched so casually.

I saw the Count lying within the box upon the earth, some of which the rude falling from the cart had scattered over him ... on the instant came the sweeping and flash of Jonathon's great [*kukri*] knife. I shrieked as I saw it shear through the throat; whilst at the same moment Mr Morris's bowie knife plunged in the heart ... before our very eyes, and almost in the drawing of a breath, the whole body crumbled into dust and passed from our sight.

Nevertheless, and despite all the other 'resurrections', in 2009, this genuine, proto-type Dracula *was* brought back to life again in *Dracula: The Un-Dead* written by Dacre Stoker (Bram Stoker's great-grandnephew) and Ian Holt in what was endorsed by The Bram Stoker Society's newsletter as "a bone-chilling sequel based on Bram Stoker's own handwritten notes for character and plot threads exercised from the original edition. Written with the blessing and co-operation of the Stoker family members, *Dracula: The Un-Dead* begins in 1912, twenty-five years after Dracula crumbled to dust." I can assure you, dear reader, that there is no power on this earth, or under it, that can resurrect a vampire once it has been despatched, which is why I steer well clear of re-enactment societies and butchers' shops!

For Dracula aficionados, there are also several suggested locations for 'Dracula's Castle' although according to Hans Corneel de Roos (*The Ultimate Dracula,*) Stoker's own hand-written research notes confirm that he had a specific mountain top location in the Transylvanian Carpathian mountains: a fictional castle on Mount Izvorul Calimanului in Transylvania, some 20 miles south-east of the Borgo Pass. But for the record the pretenders include:

- Poenari Castle: an important fortress of Vlad the Impaler but some considerable distance away from the novel's action.
- Bran Castle: is a fortress situated on the border between Transylvania and Wallachia, and although commonly known as 'Dracula's Castle' and marketed as such, there is no evidence that Stoker knew anything about it.
- Picturesque Hunyad Castle was where Vlad the Impaler was imprisoned.
- Orava Castle: the location for the filming of *Nosferatu*.

There are, of course, hundreds of other classic vampire tales that reflect the fashion of the time, which can be found in various translations and anthologies. Some are intriguingly original, others pleasant bedtime reading, while the rest are downright boring and repetitive. *The Vampire,* presented by Roger Vadim – the first director to film *Carmilla* – was an early attempt at compiling the best stories into one volume, including:

Augustine Calmet – *The Vampires of Hungary and Surrounding Countries*

Lawrence Durrell – *Carnival*

Sheridan Le Fanu – *Carmilla*

Theophile Gautier – *The Beautiful Vampire*

Edgar Allan Poe – *Berenice*

Simon Ravern – *Chriseis*

Guy de Maupassant – *The Horla*

E F Benson – *Mrs Amworth*

Sir Arthur Conan Doyle – *The Adventure of the Sussex Vampire*

Robert Bloch – *The Cloak*

Nicolai Gogol – Viy

E C Tubb – *Fresh Guy*

Luigi Capuana – *A Vampire*

Ray Bradbury – *The Man Upstairs*

Bram Stoker – *The Death of Dracula*

Many of the tales are familiar, being extracts from the novels of Stoker, Raven and Durrell, while the Calmet piece has been taken from his classic study of the vampire myth, *The Phantom World.* Other anthologies worth putting aside for bedtime reading include Alan Ryan's *Penguin Book of Vampire Stories*, Michael Parry's *The Rivals of Dracula*, Peter Haining's *The Midnight People* and *Vampire,* and Richard Dalby's *Dracula's Brood* – many of which have been adapted for cinema and television.

In marked contrast to all the other classic vampire stories, however, it is Lord Ruthven – who is rarely mentioned in the anthologies – who lives to bite another day: "The guardians hastened to protect Miss Aubrey; but when they arrived, it was too late. Lord Ruthven had disappeared, and Aubrey's sister has glutted the thirst of a VAMPYRE!" Thanks to the penmanship of the Villa Diadoti crowd I remain immortal and eternal.

Chapter Three

The Gothic Society

Those readers familiar with *The Vampyre* will be fully aware that I have no difficulty in moving in such exalted circles as social etiquette demands, and although I was considered to be somewhat of an enigma among the fashionable elite of the time, none guessed my true identity. More through curiosity than anything else, I followed the development of the vampire novel and the reactions it had on the reading public since it was often the subject of drawing room and salon small talk, and I could converse with some authority on the subject ...

"Bram Stoker's novel *Dracula* is one of the most horrifying books in English literature. It was published in May 1897, was an immediate success, and has never since been out of print. In America, where it has been published since 1899, it is still a best seller," wrote Raymond McNally in *In Search of Dracula*. And just a few days before it was published, the Count appeared on stage for the first time, in a play entitled *Dracula, or the Un-Dead*; it was solidly based on the book with a playing time was something more than four hours, and I was there on the first night. Its performance on 17th May 1897 was the only one that Stoker ever witnessed.

The innovative narrative style of the novel is unusual for its time in that it comprises of diary and journal entries, personal letters, medical records, and a ship's log. And Elizabeth Miller, Professor of English at the Memorial University of Newfoundland, observed in *Udolpho* magazine, the narrators (of which there are several) only record what they have individually experienced – such as the contents of Lucy Westenra's private correspondence that describes Dracula's *modus operandi*.

Inserted among these personal and professional correspondences are mass-media texts, sections from newspaper articles, meticulously clipped and collated. Furthermore, the process of preservation and transmission of the various pieces that comprise the text utilises many forms: notes kept in shorthand, recorded on gramophones, transcribed (in duplicate) by typewriter and sent by telegraph, leading one critic to note that for all its mediaevalism, *Dracula* is 'textually au courant', with its fusion of nineteenth century diaristic and epistolary narrative modes with cutting edge technology. We are even presented with Kodak pictures, as real estate agent Jonathan Harker brings to the medieval castle of Dracula in Transylvania a set of photographs ...

An Irish actor-manager, Hamilton Deane, tried for many years to persuade playwrights to produce another play and finally wrote one himself in 1923. The play, *Dracula*, was performed in June 1924 at the Grant Theatre in Derby and was an immediate success. On 14th February 1927, it moved to London, where it had one of the longest runs of any play in English theatrical history. Collaborating with an American writer, John L Balderston, the play opened at the Fulton Theatre in October 1927, with an unknown Hungarian actor named Bela Lugosi in the starring role. The show ran for a year on Broadway, and for two years on tour – eventually breaking all previous records for any modern play touring in the USA. While *Dracula's Guest and Other Weird Stories*, was published in 1914 by Stoker's widow although 'Dracula's Guest' was originally written for inclusion in *Dracula*, but was cut out of the initial editions.

These mouth-watering historical morsels were ambrosia to members of The Gothic Society – described as 'England's purplest literary society' it was an organisation that encouraged serious scholarship alongside outrageous costume parties in suitably Gothic locations. "Each different strand of the Gothic is represented by different members," explained its delectable organiser Jennie Gray in her welcoming letter. "They range from those who want sheer horror to those who appreciate the aesthetics of it all ... Nowadays we lead safe and secure well-ordered lies, whereas the Gothic is dark and dangerous. It is the reverse of the lives they are leading today – and people want that. Basically, the Society concerns itself with anything to do with morbid and macabre things." How I loved it when you spoke thus, dear lady!

I'm delighted to say for those few brief years I treasured my membership among like-minded souls. Founded by Jennie Gray, and her *alter ego* Edward de la Bedoyere in 1990, the Society's magazine only went as far as Volume Two before the vampires elbowed their way in. A suitably embellished book review of intrepid 1990s vampire hunter and scourge of Highgate Cemetery, Sean Manchester's factional exploits appeared – together with a resume of the current vampire societies that revealed the state (or stake) of play on the vampire scene of the time ...

Review: *The Highgate Vampire*: **AD 1990**: As 'graves give up their dead and ... the night air hideous grows with shrieks', an ever-increasing number of besotted disciples – among them some of the palest, leanest specimens known to humanity (and I use the latter word in its broadest possible sense) gather in suitably dank and gloomy establishments amidst the shrouded skeletons of the few decrepit ancestors they have failed thus far to resuscitate, there to quaff Bull's Blood, swoon over Ingrid Pitt's performance in *The Vampyre Lovers,* and place a wreath of wilted flowers upon the tomb of their undead master: DRACULA, PRINCE OF DARKNESS ... Ed.

Not so Sean Manchester ... President of the UK's only 'non-vampiroid' organisation, *The International Society for the Advancement of Irreducible Vampire and Lycanthrope Research,* (established 1970), whose occasional large newsletter, *The Cross and the Stake*, is perhaps the liveliest of the current glut of vampire-fixated publications indispensable to those who wish to keep abreast of what is *really* going on in the ghastly world of the living dead. Since the close of the sixties, when the *Hampstead & Highgate Express* posed the question 'Does a Vampire walk in Highgate Cemetery?' Manchester has waged relentless war on the species, pursuing the original abomination across North London for over a decade before finally dispatching it in true Van Helsing tradition by means of 'Bell, book and candle, stake, crucifix and garlic, Holy Water and decapitation'.

All this and much more of sephulcral aspect is recounted in his lurid case history of the haunting, *The Highgate Vampire*, an extraordinary, often ghoulish document: all leering apparitions, headless corpses, grey specters, midnight exhumations, monstrous black arachnids (well, one anyway), plunging necklines, moldy sandwiches ... The Friends of Highgate Cemetery were less than thrilled, however, at the appearance of a potboiler featuring, among other niceties, a photograph of a staked and dissolving corpse, especially as it belonged to a former patron of their hallowed grounds, and consequently picketed local booksellers in a successful bid to have his unofficial guide to this Victorian Valhalla, *The Vampire Tour*, withdrawn from sale ...

The Sean Manchester crusade appeared in a number of volumes – each episode more ludicrous than the next – but it all added to the fun and vampires ruled the literary scene in the popularity stakes. While under the pen-name of 'Scavenger's Daughter' we were introduced to the various vampire societies that existed at home and abroad, although I subsequently discovered them to be less fun than The Gothic Society crowd who re-introduced the spirit of decadence into their proceedings, if not the actuality.

In the early 1990s there were two organizations operating under the banner of **The Vampyre Society**, with each denouncing the other and claiming to be the 'real thing'.

The first, operated by Carole Bohanan, produced a quarterly journal, *The Velvet Vampire*, an impressive glossy publication, strong on graphics and layout if sometimes lacking in literary content. While the other **Vampire Society's** quarterly, *For the Blood is the Life*, edited by Allen J Gittens was promising to pull the corpse-fat out of the fire with a special 'Third Anniversary' issue. Meetings were the *raison d'etre* of the famous and ultra-conservative **Dracula Society** (founded 1970); membership is by the approval of the committee, so it is advisable to bone up on much that is gothic-terror-romantic before applying.

There were several American Vampire Societies listed such as **The Count Dracula Fan Club** (not to be confused with John Raven's London-based organisation of the same name which ceased to exist in a blaze of controversy earlier this century); **The Lucy Westenra Society of the Undead**; **Vampire Information Exchange**, etc., "but that's a whole new goblet of grave worms, and one of which I am largely ignorant," wrote the delightful Ms Gray. Lastly, the **Vampire Research Centre**, which in the summer of 1995, claimed to have 1,215 real vampires on its books following the release of Coppola's *Dracula*; while hot on the heels of the cinematic version of *Interview With Vampire*, several 'came out' to give interviews to the tabloid press. I did have the opportunity of proving to some of these film buffs that they weren't *real* vampires after all!

As far as the Gothic Society was concerned, however, the costume parties were a great favourite with the members, and the first I attended, which also caught the imagination of the press was the 'Summer Party' in the reptile house at London Zoo on 26th July 1991, where "decadent aesthetes chat with Byron look-alikes." It was a far cry from the first proposed social event, however, as Jennie Gray explained, "When we advertised our

Black Banquet (an incident taken from J K Huysman's decadent novel *Against Nature*) in the *Spectator*, we had a lot of interest from men. Of course, they knew that in the book the all-black banquet is served by naked negresses, but we couldn't quite manage that."

In reality the idea was based on the mock funeral supper held by Des Esseintes for his lost virility, and guests were implored to come dressed in the spirit of the occasion – "elegantly and in black, although they may add little frivolities to their black garb if they wish, such as ties for the gentlemen and ribbons for the ladies in blood red, altar lily white, and arsenic green ..." Sadly the Black Banquet never came to pass but it was the thought that counted – instead members made do with a supper at Newstead Abbey, held in the honour of Dr John Polidori – and to celebrate the publication of *The Vampyre & Other Works*. I also attended this event, dressed exactly as I am described in Polidor's novella, although I am less stand-offish now than I was portrayed way back then.

To my great delight, one of the Society's first publications was this two-volume set of Dr Polidori's *The Vampyre*, a copy of the 1816 original – which was hailed as a welcome addition to the resurgent Gothic boom. I still have my copy of this slim volume, although much dog-eared and well travelled. Two hundred years previously the Gothic novel had been hugely popular: from Horace Walpole's *The Castle of Otranto* (1764) and Ann Radcliffe's *The Mysteries of Udolpho* (1794) to Charles R Maturin's *Melmoth the Wander* (1820), this had been the most successful literary sub-genre of the 18th and 19th centuries. By the early 20th century these stories of 'romantic horror' had declined almost to the point of extinction, but within a few years publishers started looking into their back catalogues, and long-forgotten titles, once of interest only to collectors and academics, were being reprinted and aimed at the general reader.

The first contributors' summer party I attended was a rather an unusual affair, where contributors and artists gathered together in a vaulted cellar in Greenwich. To the strains of a string quartet, 'vamps', mini-lords in linen shirts, and ladies in black velvet, revealed their identities as the ones responsible for sharing their strange peccadilloes with the rest of the membership. Friendships were made and the following year we found ourselves interred in the same cool vaulted cellar, while the rest of London sweltered in the heat – until there was a bomb scare and the place was evacuated. It caused some consternation in the pub opposite when a whole party of vampire-like creatures materialised in the public bar in full regalia – and in brilliant sunlight too!

This 'leading society for the study of macabre, morbid and black-hued themes', allowed the vampires to reappear in force in Volume Nine, and created a good-natured schism between 'the aesthetes and the vampires'. Not only was there another interview with 'vampire hunter' Sean Manchester; the issue contained essays on Stoker's *Dracula* and Le Fanu; a tale of the vampire of Père Lachaise, and a spoof 'On the Vampire as a Family pet'. Needless to say, the Society was often the focus for strange requests for meetings from a Gothic sub-culture whose intensions were 'bluer' than even the 'purplest' members were ready for.

On the flip-side, one of the first 'serious' studies of the vampire came from the indomitable and irrepressible Montague Summers, who was never one to miss an opportunity when it came to demonstrating his expertise on the subject of the Devil's children. In the following extract from *The Vampire* – his collection of research originally published in 1928 – he defines his 'monster' in his customary hell-fire preacher bombast:

He is gaunt and lean with a hideous countenance and eyes wherein are glinting the red fire of perdition. When, however, he has satiated his lust for warm human blood his body becomes horribly puffed and bloated, as though he were some great leech gorged and replete to bursting. Cold as ice or it may be fevered and burning as hot coal, the skin is deathly pale, but the lips are very full, rich and red; the teeth white and gleaming and the canine teeth wherewith he bites deep into the neck of his prey to suck hence the vital streams which reanimate his body and invigorate all his forces appear notably sharp and pointed. Often his mouth curls back in a vulpine snarl which bares these fangs ...

With the growing popularity of the vampire cult, Senate Paperback Reprint re-issued a new version of the original in 1995, which was eagerly reviewed in *Udolpho* magazine for the benefit of its members – and not altogether favourably, since it was totally anti everything we held dear!

For eight and a half years we relished these quarterly offerings in a magazine that forced the reader to re-visit old Gothic favourites mouldering on the book shelves and rekindle the love of fine prose and vampiric musings. Then it was all over – from the winter issue of 1998 the Society breathed its last. Jennie Gray penned her funeral oration in the last edition of the magazine and former members were left clutching their tattered copies of *The Vampyre* for solace. Nevertheless, the spirit of The Gothic Society lived on in the undiluted delights of the genre, the upholding of the classic vampire tradition, and the lament of the elderly that 'things aren't like when I was a vamp-let!'

Fortunately, there *were* contemporary writers who could fill the buckled shoes of their predecessors to produce comparable prose and decadent musings – and the most talented of all being Simon Raven. Described as having "the mind of a cad and the pen of an angel", his unashamed credo was "a robust eighteenth-century paganism ..." and his cruel delight in the outrageous, and lack of moralising or sentiment, are characteristics which pervade his writings. He also had a marked fascination for the supernatural that first manifested in an early novel *Doctors Wear Scarlet* (1960), which was cited by Karl Edward Wagner (himself an award-winning American writer, poet, editor and publisher of horror and writer of numerous dark fantasy and horror stories), as one of the thirteen best supernatural novels. These Gothic themes became stronger in Raven's later works such as *The Roses of Picardie* (1980), *September Castle* (1983), parts of the *Alms For Oblivion* and the *First-Born of Egypt* sequence, and the vampire novella *The Islands of Sorrow* (1994).

Doctors Wear Scarlet is set against Raven's customary background of academia and University life, and has a distinctly macabre and spine-chilling theme. It starts harmlessly enough with a young man's infatuation for a beautiful Greek girl, but Chriseis is no ordinary holiday love affair. In a location so familiar to me on my travels, three friends track down their missing companion across the Aegean, where it becomes increasingly obvious that their relationship is strange to say the least.

> She was from the ancient world all right, but she was from a part of it he didn't know about. Something he had overlooked in his investigations. Something which has persisted through the ages, firstly in Greece, where it had its birth and where it is still strongest, but later in all of Europe. She was the votary of a cult very different from those, whether good or evil, with which Richard Fountain had concerned himself ...she's a woman all right, and she's a mortal woman. But she is the inheritress, if I'm not mistaken, of an old and particularly obscene tradition ...

Despite despatching Chriseis in the remote mountains of Crete and not without cost to themselves, the missing scholar is returned to his University – but the curse of the vampire is never far behind and with it comes the inevitable conclusion. In true neo-Gothic tradition, his characters reflect no sense of moralising or sentiment, but with a mischievous and cruel delight in the outrageous. Raven's characters re-introduced the true spirit of decadence into the 20th century.

The Islands of Sorrow features another familiar Raven backdrop of Venice and in true Gothic style, is full of decay and suppuration – although the un-dead in this novella are completely different to the traditional variety. The action takes place solely at a table in a restaurant with one diner telling a story to his friend about some strange events that occurred in Venice some years previously. The narrative takes us on a quest through dank slimy tunnels, forty yards of pitch darkness that led into windowless squares, along narrow streets with houses on either side that the tops of the houses formed another tunnel that led to catacombs beneath a crumbling fortress where the reader encountered the un-dead. This was Simon Raven's last book but it was a fitting end – and if Arthur Machen had been hailed as the High Priest of Gothic Horror, then Simon Raven was certainly its Crown Prince.

This burgeoning Gothic revival did not, however, please all members of the Gothic Society. As the journalist who covered the Summer Party at the Reptile House had observed at the start: "They welcomed the wider availability of the books, but did not want everyone identifying with the genre; they would rather keep it to themselves rather than have it degraded by modern creations." Or as one member is quoted as saying: "It should be limited to intellectuals. Once everybody becomes decadent, there is no point anymore."

A sentiment with which both Simon Raven and myself would whole-heartedly agree.

Chapter Four

Ladies in Black Velvet

In view of some of my preceding comments, readers may begin to think me a touch misogynistic but do rest assured that I am a seasoned 'lady killer'. When you have lived as long as I have, there have been many women but few linger in the memory down through the ages. Suffice to say that I have become a widower several times over! But believe it or not, I remember one who resembled the fair Greek Ianthe rather than those with the cloned drawing-room charms of Miss Aubrey, or with the overly rampant sexual allure of the later cinema sirens.

By and large, the characters of vampire legend are generally literary inventions, despite the fact that many claim to be centuries old – but, along with Vlad the Impaler, there is also authentic historical documentation concerning a real-life 17th-century Hungarian Countess: Elizabeth Bathory. Born in 1560, she belonged to one of the oldest and wealthiest families in Transylvania and the McNally-Florescu investigations (*In Search of Dracula*) revealed the possibility of a tenuous link between the Bathory and the Dracula families.

While her soldier-husband was away fighting, the Countess was busy cultivating the acquaintance of local occultists and witches and, on his death, her atrocities began in earnest. Afraid of losing her beauty, this authentic mistress of the macabre misguidedly indulged in regular 'blood-baths' provided by a blood-draining ritual that over a ten-year period cost the lives of over 50 young local girls. One of her intended victims escaped and raised the alarm about the 'gruesome goings-on' at the castle and a raid was authorised for the night of 30th December 1610.

Not surprisingly, everyone implicated in the murders, except for Countess herself, were executed; Elizabeth Bathory was never formally convicted of any crime. Instead, she was sealed up in her bedchamber, with all the doors and windows bricked up, with only a small hole through which food could be passed. In *Countess Dracula*, author Tony Thorne refutes this part of the legend, and claims that she was merely confined and isolated from society. Nevertheless, four years later, in 1614, she was found dead by one of her gaolers, whether from natural causes or poison, we will never know.

Like Vlad the Impaler, the Countess was not technically a vampire, but it is the statuesque, tawny-haired Ingrid Pitt with the 'exotic looks and intriguing accent' who is remembered as playing the title role in the film *Countess Dracula* (1971), which was based on the legends surrounding Elizabeth Báthory, rather than historical accuracy. It was Ms Pitt's work with Hammer Film Productions that elevated her to cult figure status, beginning with the starring role of Carmilla/Mircalla in *The Vampire Lovers* (1970), based on Le Fanu's novella – and the later publication of *The Ingrid Pitt Bedside Companion for Vampire Lovers* (1998).

In *Carmilla*, however, the baser side of the vampire's nature comes to the fore in a form of overt lesbianism, and in direct contrast to *Dracula* where the victims reveal a distinct heterosexual tendency, Carmilla only targets females for her attentions. Neither is she very discreet about her intension, since even the sheltered Laura is in no doubt as to her desire.

> Sometimes after an hour of apathy, my strange and beautiful companion would take my hand and hold it with a fond pressure, renewed again and again; blushing softly, gazing in my face with languid and burning eyes, and breathing so fast that her dress rose and fell with the tumultuous respiration. It was like the ardour of a lover; it embarrassed me; it was hateful and yet overpowering ...

Le Fanu chose to add a brief history of his captivating creation and we learn that having followed her home from her first ball a vampire accosted 'our heroine' in her bed later that night. A mysterious 'Moravian nobleman' who in his early youth, had been a "passionate and favoured lover" of Mircalla/Carmilla and, knowing the circumstances surrounding her death, had somewhat misguidedly concealed her tomb so that she should not suffer the final indignities of beheading and burning. Perhaps Carmilla became disenchanted with the perfidious male who had originally caused her condition, and decided to create a female companion for her twilight world – although there is scant evidence to suggest that the General's niece was ever cast as a potential candidate for that role. Or perhaps Carmilla merely found child and female victims easier to manage.

Dracula's ladies were of a more robust constitution, however, and also imbued with supernatural powers of transportation as Jonathan Harker discovers:

> Then I began to notice that there were some quaint little specks floating in the rays of the moonlight. They were like the tiniest grains of dust, and they whirled around and gathered in clusters in a nebulous sort of way. I watched them with a sense of soothing, and a sort of calm stole over me ... I was becoming hypnotised! Quicker and quicker danced the dust, and the moonbeams seemed to quiver as they went by me into the mass of gloom beyond. More and more they gathered till they seemed to take dim phantom shapes ... were those of the three ghostly women to whom I was doomed ...

Having followed Dracula back to Transylvania, Van Helsing encounters them in another manifestation.

> Even in the dark there was a light of some kind, as there ever is over snow; and it seemed as though the snow-flurries and

the wreaths of mist took shape as of women with trailing garments ... At the first coming of the dawn the horrid figures melted in the whiling mist and snow; the wraiths of transparent gloom moved away towards the castle, and were lost.

There is also a barely suppressed sexual tension in the character of Lucy Westenra as she flirts and teases her three suitors, and we are left in no doubt as to why Dracula chose her first, rather than the limpid Mina, even though Van Helsing describes the latter as a "pearl among women." As Lucy's fiancé is about to drive the stake home through her heart, Dr Seward observes that he can "see its dint in the white flesh" – which suggests that Lucy is bared to the waist, under the eyes of her admirers. In fact, there is something of a ravishment about her final death and it is her intended husband who carries out the deed; much more gory than Dracula's actual departure from this world at the end of the novel.

The Thing in the coffin writhed; and a hideous, blood-curdling screech came from the opened red lips. The body shook and quivered and twisted in wild contortions; the sharp white teeth clamped together till the lips were cut and the mouth was smeared with a crimson foam. But Arthur never faulted ... as his untrembling arm rose and fell, driving deeper and deeper the mercy-bearing stake, whilst blood from the pierced heart welled and spurted up around it ...

In subsequent novels (and films), many of the female vampires were often a sorry lot. There was a lot of sexual allure and bosom heaving, but generally speaking they trailed about like exotic hens that have been caught out in a thunderstorm, but thankfully there were still one or two around to carry on the tradition. In *Doctors Wear Scarlet* (1960), the exquisitely beautiful Chriseis was a breath of familiar air and quickly demonstrated her powers of hypnotic suggestion when she returns to claim her lover. Having been driven out into the storm by his friends, this was no wet hen that returned.

> I saw that the door was half open, and that just inside it was standing a woman, dressed in black trousers and a kind of black above them. She also had on a medium length black cape, which was held together in front by a short gold chain ...I saw with great clarity every detail of her dress and her appearance ... that on her throat just above the gold chain which secured her cloak, was a small silver brooch; that her black hair was long and very glossy in appearance for a woman who had just spent the night in the open and many days living in extreme discomfort; that her complexion was white yet healthy, her nose well proportioned, her forehead narrow; that her chin was delicate; and that her eyes were bright ... It was these bight eyes that were fixed on me now ... Sometimes the light caught her brooch and it would flash; sometimes it caught her eyes, which then became brighter than ever ...

Unusually, Chriseis is despatched by strangulation although the precaution of hammering a stake through her heart is also deemed necessary. Nevertheless, her image continues to haunt her lover's mind, and he continues to speak about her a though she was still alive: right up until the end. Which is rather intriguing because when we first meet her in the narrative, she's also wearing 'wellies', which is hardly a 'glam vamp' accessory – and yet it does not in any way detract from her sinister or captivating presence. Like the character of Rebecca in the novel of the same name, Chriseis continues to dominate the story long after she is dead.

Another sultry beauty worthy of note is Barbara, Count Kotor's vampire daughter in *The Vampires of Alfama* (1975) by

Pierre Kast, and an even more alarming creature. A 'magnificent gossamer blonde', she is highly intelligent, coldly calculating and we know that even when under attack by the Inquisition that she *will* survive …

> Her special gift, which she had received as her share, was the strength of magnetic and hypnotic suggestion, a subject of endless discussions with her father. He accepted only the absolute conscious, determined and convinced participation of disciples. On several occasions Barbara used her power to suck the blood of boys and girls who were more victims than accomplices. When Kotor found out he went mad with rage. In vain she mocked his moral values. He kept to them; severity marked all his actions. And Barbara's behaviour, although he found it immoral above everything else, was also the source of a grave peril, linked with the source of the age-old terror inspired by the vampires.

With her brother dead and her father on his way to the New World, Barbara remains behind in Alfama and there is surely a wonderful opportunity here for a sequel that would in no way detract from the original story. The most erotic scenes in the book belong to Barbara and we are left in no doubt that she uses her body and mind to ensnare her willing victims. Kast has created a vampire being with life in its veins, set against a backdrop of terror-inspired medievalism that would endure for centuries – a contemporary perhaps of Catherine Deneuve's portrayal of the 20th-century Miriam Blaylock in the cult-classic *The Hunger*.

The female influence in Anne Rice's *Interview With The Vampire* (1976) takes an unusual twist, in producing what is probably the most terrifying female vampire of all time – Claudia. Created in one of Lestat's more perverse moments, this five-year-old child has all the captivating appeal of a beautiful doll, combined with the deadliness of her adult kind.

"See her, Louis, how plump and sweet she looks, as if even death can't take her freshness; the will to live is too strong! He might make a sculpture of her tiny lips and rounded hands, but he cannot make her fade! ... She was the most beautiful child I'd ever seen, and now she glowed with the cold fire of a vampire. Her eyes were a woman's eyes, I could see it already. She would become white and spare like us but not lose her shape ..."

It's not until Louis begins to educate Claudia and her intellect develops that she questions Lestat about the existence of other vampires, which puts their *ménage a trois* under threat. Although she remains the same physically, Louis slowly becomes aware of the subtle changes: "There was something dreadfully sensual about her lounging on the settee in a tiny nightgown of lace and stitched pearls; she became an eerie and powerful seductress ..." She studied books of the occult, of witches and witchcraft, and of vampires when she realises that Lestat cannot answer her questions – he has no answers and they are locked together in a battle of hate-inspired wills.

It's not until this woman-child utters the words: *"The sleep of sixty-five years has ended!"* that we realise the enormity of Lestat's actions. Here is a mature woman with all its passions and emotions, crushed into the tiny body of a five-year-old girl, and we finally understand the depth of Claudia's hatred for Lestat. It was Louis who first drank her blood, but it was Lestat who turned her into a vampire. Not surprisingly, the character re-appears in other volumes of the *Vampire Chronicles: The Vampire Lestat, The Queen of the Damned, The Tale of the Body Thief, The Vampire Armand* and *Merrick*. Perhaps, in the entire history of the vampire, *this* is the genre's most perverted scenario of all.

The ultimate and most fascinating in contemporary female vampires, however, must be surely be found in Whitley Strieber's *The Hunger* (1981) in which a beautiful and wealthy

Miriam Blaylock, takes human lovers and transforms them into vampires.

Like myself, Miriam is from the ancient world but due to some genetic malfunction, her lovers do not share her longevity and when her latest companion suddenly begins to show signs of aging, she attempts to find a cure from a brilliant young research scientist who may hold the key to immortality. Not surprisingly, having been promised eternal life – which has only lasted 200 years – her latest paramour becomes resentful and uncontrollable; threatening the security of their life-style when John kills 13-year-old Alice whom Miriam is grooming to take his place, and has to be dealt with ...

Set against a backdrop of modern, up-town New York, the Blaylock's live in a state of subdued luxury behind an armoury of sophisticated security systems. The action is a kaleidoscope of flashbacks to the ancient world, the evidence of which are carefully preserved in the attic. For here are the remains of all her past loves, dried, desiccated bodies, whose spirits, nevertheless, continue to endure as whispering shadows of their former selves. From the onset of John's ageing process, Miriam prepares his final resting place – a carbon fibre steel coffin sealed with twelve bolts that could be closed and locked in a matter of seconds – and we finally get to understand what a remorseless and accomplished killer she is.

Strangely enough, I found the refrain of distant memory resonating in Strieber's narrative in that vampires often seek out their own kind, but operate more safely living a solitary existence. There are also the heightened senses that picked up the vibrations of Life from the tiniest moth to the sweeping movement of the stars. Miriam's need for constant companionship, I think I may honestly say, is a female trait echoed in the attentions of Carmilla – the male of the species moves fastest who hunts alone. It is this choice of wanting (or needing) companionship that proves to be the downfall of the majority of vampires, and one I almost learned to my own cost many centuries ago.

By comparison, for sheer amusement on a very personal level, *The Merciful Women* (2000) by Federico Andahazi introduces a completely different kind of vampire, albeit in a direct return to the Gothic literary genre. The two Legrand sisters were beautiful vaudeville performers in their day but the years have passed and they can no longer attract young, virile suitors needed to sustain their unusual 'life-support' requirements. For there is a mysterious third sister who maintains control over the life and death of the triplets and another way must be found to acquire the male 'elixir' necessary for their existence.

> I am indeed a monster – and I don't mean metaphorically ... I suffer from a sort of chemical abnormality, from an unknown physiological quirk that has turned me into an amorphous freak. It is as if I were the residue from the formation of my sister ... It was only to be expected that the malignant chemistry that shaped my physiognomy would also shape my soul in the image of the body it inhabited. Par from my naturally coarse disposition, which is closer to that of a wild beast than a lady, I lack any attributes that might be described as delicate.

Nevertheless, despite her deformities, Annette Legrande is blessed with a wry sense of humour – as we discover when she describes the sexual antics of her ageing sisters – *and* literary talent. The story is set against the backdrop of the Villa Diadoti and paints a rather unflattering portrait of each of the real-life characters who took part in the unfolding drama. There is also a nightmare quality about *The Merciful Women* in that the narrative twists and turns to produce a new horror around every corner, but always tempered with a sense of the ridiculous or impossible. The conclusion matches the earthy sense of humour worthy of Lord Byron himself! Andahazi has given us a fascinating prequel to *The Vampyre* and leaves his own indelible mark on 21st century Gothic literature for many years to come.

Despite the early creation of *Carmilla*, and apart from those mentioned in this chapter, there are few female vampires that can hold their own against the male of the species for sheer ruthlessness. Pouting lips and heaving bosoms aren't enough to keep a 'vamp' alive for centuries and many of the women were mere 'cannon fodder' for the ultimate gory despatches required by the genre. Nevertheless, those few female vampires that *have* been created to endure, remain un-dead in all their glory!

Chapter Five

"Enter freely and of your own will!"

Needless to say, the contacts I'd made during all those Grand Tours stood me in good stead when I reached England. The introductions gave me access to the wives, sweethearts and sisters of those young men whose company I'd sought in Italy, France and Greece. I was considered to be fascinating and exotic, and since the touch of the vampire allowed for seduction without dishonour, I was able to pleasure those young ladies of noble birth in secret. The vampire's kiss is not always deadly, and the smallest sip can be likened to savouring a glass of fine wine, without the urge to consume the whole bottle.

Nevertheless, almost everyone who reads *The Vampyre* and *Dracula* is struck by the latent sexuality encoded in the text, where a pure woman is pursued and seduced by a sexually aggressive male. But as the good Professor Miller observes, the central sexual agenda of the text is somewhat different: the threat that Dracula poses is the manner in which he makes it possible for a female sexuality to manifest that is so abhorrent to Van Helsing – "in that the vampire can transform chaste women into sexually ravenous beasts." While Judith Weissman notes in her article 'Women and Vampires: Dracula as a Victorian Novel': "[Dracula] is the man whom all other men fear, the man who can, without any loss of freedom or power himself, seduce other men's women and make them sexually insatiable with a performance that the others cannot match." I would not class myself in the role of rival to the Count, but it is true that women cannot resist our advances and I have had my moments.

'The Curse of the Unread' also examined the sexual elements that are more than evident in the encounter Jonathan Harker has with Dracula's harem of vampire ladies. Who feature in the book, suggests Tina Rath, to 'preserve the proprieties', since Dracula is never depicted drinking blood from a male victim. "Whatever we may speculate about the crew of the ill-fated 'Demeter', while even Lucy's child victims are described as male when their sex is actually specified, so blood-drinking is essentially a heterosexual activity throughout the *Dracula* text." I must add that I have never felt the urge to drink the blood of a male, all that pumping testosterone I would find distinctively unpalatable!

Of course Stoker was fully aware of the sexual dynamics generated by the act of blood-drinking and Harker frankly acknowledges the perverse attraction of the deadly harem: "All three had brilliant white teeth that shone like pearls against the ruby of their voluptuous lips … I felt in my heart a wicked, burning desire that they would kiss me with those red lips." It is also evident from the two pages of thinly veiled eroticism that Harker is about to become a willing victim if he doesn't engage his wits and get the hell out of there.

Dracula's ladies are given subtle identities of their own in that the two brunettes have great, dark piercing eyes and high aquiline noses, like their Master, with the suggestion that perhaps they are some distant relation. The third is fair with great, wavy masses of golden hair and eyes like sapphires; their laughter is silvery and musical with an underlying "intolerable, tingling sweetness." While Dracula's breath is described as "rank", his blonde mistress's breath is described as "sweet it was in one sense, honey-sweet, and sent the same tingling through the nerves as her voice, but with a bitter underlying the sweet, a bitter offensiveness, as one smells in blood."

In the television ad man's mind, it's a wonder that this scene hasn't appeared as a Listerine advertisement.

Still on the subject of sex, Rath gives an even more fascinating equation of vampirism with sexual love when Dracula intervenes to rescue Harker from them. The blonde vampire, who is presumably a favourite of the Count and who has the more elaborate tomb, taunts him with the words: "You yourself never loved; you never love" and his soft reply suggests that it was his 'love' that turned them into vampires: "Yes, I too can love; you yourselves can tell it from the past." Unlike the Count, I have always avoided permanent relationships because of the complications it brings in being responsible for one who has not learned to survive the trials and tribulations of being un-dead. Besides, it would be a rare woman indeed, with whom one would wish to spend eternity.

Nevertheless, even the elderly and almost puritanical Van Helsing is not immune to these female charms as his encounter with the first of the ladies of Castle Dracula reveals. "She lay in her Vampire sleep, so full of life and voluptuous beauty that I shudder as though I have come to do murder ... There is some fascination, surely, when I am moved by the mere presence of such a one, even lying as she lay in a tomb fretted with age and heavy with the dust of centuries ... Yes, I was moved – I, Van Helsing, with all my purpose and with my motive for hate ..." Despite the fact that he despatches each one of the three females with cool precision, he is conscious aware of what he describes as 'butcher work' and when all three are gone to dust, he can find pity in his heart from the "very instinct of man in me, which call some of my sex to love and to protect ..."

Duncan Barford's comments in *Udolopho* magazine suggested that vampires represent the bestial, sexual side of human nature but "... the truly Gothic rests upon uncertainty and a fine balance between that which is conscious, and that which has been repressed. Decline and depravity are always just around the next corner, yet are tenuously hidden, barely held in check by the existing rotten order ..." I would suggest, however, that people feel embarrassed by any admission that they find a certain erotic stimulation in the supernatural elements of the vampire. There have been far more human abominations throughout history, than in a creature that finds itself in the unenviable position of having to drink human blood in order to exist. The 'fine balance' is immaterial when your very 'being' is at stake – not all of us chose to become vampires, and most had no choice in the matter. Having evolved naturally like Darwin's survival of the fittest by adapting and acclimatising ourselves to our condition, we merely exist on the natural level of predator – the only difference being that our prey is human not animal.

Le Fanu introduced another forbidden element in order to make the exquisite Carmilla abhorrent to ordinary, decent Victorian readers. In the novel, youth and loneliness, make Laura vulnerable and Le Fanu "overtly uses lesbianism, which was not only a taboo subject at the time, but which had all sorts of evil connotations, to heighten tension and to symbolise abnormality." Nevertheless, the reader needs to appreciate her victim's reaction to such an approach, since Carmilla is obviously blessed with the vampire's ability to fascinate and hypnotise:

From these foolish embraces, which were not of very frequent occurrence, I must allow, I used to wish to extricate myself; but my energies seemed to fail me. Her murmured words sounded like a lullaby in my ear, and soothed my resistance into a trance, from which I only seemed to recover myself when she withdrew her arms … I experienced a strange tumultuous excitement that was pleasurable, ever and anon, mingled with a vague sense of fear and disgust. I had no distinct thoughts about her while such scenes lasted, but I was conscious of a love growing into adoration, and also of abhorrence. This I know is paradox, but I can make no other attempt to explain the feeling.

As the delectable Jennie Grey observed in the June 1992 issue of The Gothic Society's magazine:

The predatory male gallant, the ravisher and abductor, played a large part in Gothic fiction, though with the exception of the lurid *The Monk* and its imitators, sex was always out of focus in soft pastel, hinted at discreetly rather than flaunted openly. The Gothic novel achieved the highest degree of oblique lovemaking, of steamy twilight passages which walked with consummate art the borderline between suggestiveness and eroticism. Mary Wollstonecraft understood this perfectly when she wrote 'Ignorant women, forced to be chaste to preserve their reputation, allow their imagination to revel in the unnatural and meretricious ...'

The sexual allure of the vampire, however, also goes back to the beginning of history to the merging of the Sumerian *lilitu* (a demon and was often depicted as subsisting on the blood of babies), Mesopotamian myths about succubae called *lilin*, and the daughters of Lilith, the *lilu* from Hebrew demonology. Like many other aspects of Christian doctrine, absorption of Rabbinical lore and myths from other classical sources led early scholars to interpret old beliefs in a completely different and sometimes contradictory light. The basis for acceptance of the incubus/succubus/vampire legend originated with Lilith, a Hebrew deity, whose antecedents can be traced back to 3,000 BC Sumeria. With the spread of the mono-Semitic culture, however, she, like many of her kind, joined the ranks of demons.

Hebrew tradition claims that Lilith attacks men who are sleeping alone, seducing them in their dream and drinking their blood; it is this aspect of Lilith, which is most prominent in the legends about her. She is identified as mother of the incubi and succubi, and originator of the vampire myth, in that both entities are charged with drawing the lifeforce from their human victims. The incubus-succubus, like its cousin the vampire, is very much a creature of the ancient world. Unlike the vampire, however, who has been preserved with an aura of glamour within the realms of literature, folklore and superstition, the existence of the succubus was given credence by the early Church to explain away the illicit sexual activities (nocturnal or otherwise) of cloistered monks and nuns.

Incubi (male) and succubi (female) were seen as emissaries of the Devil and innumerable discussions took place during the Middle Ages about the 'corporeal manifestation' of such demonic entities that haunted the night-dreams of supposedly god-fearing men and women. The original concept, taken from Rabbinical lore and classical mythology were absorbed into Christian doctrine and by the 13th century the learned men of Rome conceded that such creatures really did exist! Church scholars came up with the theory that succubi seduced males in order to procure their semen, and then turned themselves into incubi to impregnate their female victims.

The early Church also amassed (allegedly to support the charges of heresy, witchcraft and consorting with demons) one of the greatest collections of legal pornography. And since members of the clergy, high and low, spent a considerable amount of time discussing, debating, cross-examining, writing, reading, copying, dictating and learning about such highly charged manifestations, it is hardly surprising that their nights were spent in a state of lascivious excitement and receptive to the vampiric attentions of their night-dreams.

From the beginning of the existence of the vampire in Gothic literature, there remains the barely suppressed undertones of rampant sexuality that have persisted in vampire stories to the present day. The fiend, whether based on Lord Ruthven, *Dracula* or *Carmilla*, is a charismatic creature, capable of drawing willing victims like moths to a flame. In *The Vampyre*, the assignation with the young Italian girl is thwarted by Aubrey, but on his return to Rome following his travels in Greece, he discovered that "she had not been heard of since the departure of his lordship" – the lure *is* irresistible.

When looking beneath the veneer of Stoker's *Dracula*, however, we find a much more complex creature than one who (like myself) merely required fresh human blood to maintain its existence. As Patrick McGrath observed in his article 'Bram Stoker and his Vampire': that there was "all that was good and proper on the one hand, rapt fascination with the idea of evil on the other, specifically its personification in a monstrous figure of unrestrained lust and satanic ambition."

Dracula's imitators are mere ciphers, in that they have adopted many of the Count's characteristic dislike of garlic, sunlight and crucifixes but not his far-reaching ambition. Although Count Kotor's vampires in *The Vampires of Alfama* surrendered willingly to a similar fate, as ultimate evil personified, Dracula intension was to take over the world by eliminating the distinction between life and death and create a race of vampires in his own likeness – and was not repeated until Stephen King wrote *Salem's Lot*. And what better way to pollute the human race than by seducing its women and turning them into 'creatures of voracious appetite'. McGrath observes:

> Evil on this diabolical scales demands opposition of more-than-heroic proportions; Stoker manages a masterly fusion of the medieval romance tradition with the Victorian cult of manliness ... necessary if Dracula's wickedness is to be seen in it true light, that the vampire be a match for not one but four of the finest flowers of Christian manhood that western civilisation can muster, plus of course the encyclopaedic knowledge of Van Helsing.

Unfortunately, and with true human perverseness, the modern reader finds the constant harping on about 'piety, virility, chivalry and tact' of the four heroes rather tedious. The *real* attraction is for the one who can "control a pack of wolves simply by raising his hand", or "arouse the uncontrolled female passion of unconscious desires". Needless to say, it is the latter that Dracula's enemies find most distressing, and the one element that has haunted the memory of that real-life vampire proto-type – Lord Byron.

Even Anne Rice couldn't resist the Byronic allure when introducing Armand, the handsome, auburn-haired, black-eyed head of the Parisian vampire community. Despite his active participation in the murder of a young naked woman for the entertainment of the human audience at the Théâtre des Vampires ... not to mention ordering the summary execution of Claudia, he wasn't without his own fascination ...

Someone was near, on the periphery of my vision; someone who had outsmarted my hearing, my keen anticipation, which penetrated like a sharp antenna even this distraction, or so I thought. But there he was, soundless, beyond the curtained entrance of the box, that vampire with the auburn hair, that detached one ... He would have startled me, except for his stillness, the remote dreamy quality of his expression.

Although he claimed to be the 'oldest living vampire in the world' – four-hundred years old and a 'master' vampire to boot – Rice has him trailing around after Louis like an infatuated adolescent. From the point of Claudia's death, the whole narrative becomes 'unconvincing' as Armand is reduced to a mere cipher in a story that staggers unsuccessfully towards its conclusion. Louis's perpetual angst becomes almost as tedious as the constant harping on about the virtues of the four heroes of *Dracula*!

By contrast, in *The Merciful Women*, Federico Andahazi's vampiress is constant and unflinching in her pursuit of 'human male fluids' as the author so nicely puts it. This fictional tale with a twist involving the illustrious gathering at the Villa Diodati – focuses on John Polidori, a hanger-on whose presence is merely tolerated by the literary 'greats'. In order to win the famous 'ghost story competition' he enters into 'a Faustian pact' with an elusive pen-friend, Annette Legrand, who promises to produce the most compelling vampire tale ever written in exchange for a nightly supply of fresh semen! The novel is written in the Romantic style and shies away from graphic description, while creating a candidly erotic, if at times highly hilarious, narrative.

The bi-sexual theme that often permeates the genre, especially in movie versions, alters the concept of vampire sexuality out of all proportion. For the vampire, drinking the blood of a living human is the means to stay alive and the 'prey' that is the easiest to overcome is, generally speaking, a woman or a child. A male vampire, unless circumstances are desperate, does not want to fight for his supper when seduction achieves the same result. Apart from Dracula's brief blaze of bloodlust when Harker cuts himself shaving, the Count is quite content to leave his guest to the seductive charms of his ladies. Lucy, in her new-found 'Bloofer lady' persona preys on children – although if left alone in Mina's company, who is to say that she would not have attempted to feed off her closest friend, without lesbian tendencies being introduced into the equation.

Today's vampire genre has evolved into youthful angst, designer stubble and an overt sexuality of all permutations – conditions that would never have occurred to the suave but deadly nobleman of the Gothic era. For the purist, however, the Byronic stereotype has never lost its allure and for the aficionado of the traditional vampire cult, they still prefer them 'mad, bad and dangerous to know'!

Chapter Six

Children of the Night

The vampire is one of Nature's supreme predators, albeit of a supernatural disposition; we merely hunt to satisfy our hunger although this sentiment would sit uncomfortably with the urban reader of the 21st century. Even turning the clock back one or two hundred years, when mankind roamed the earth killing animals to satisfy *his* primordial urge, we – the blue ribbon holders of the chase – were viewed as an abomination. To quote Stoker: "I heard, as if from down below in the valley, the howling of many wolves. The Count's eyes gleamed, and he said: "'Listen to them – the children of the night. What music they make! ... Ah, sir, you dwellers in the city cannot enter into the feelings of the hunter.'"

It goes without saying, that the vampire has an affinity with the canine race – more closely with hunting hounds where I originate from – especially if they were native to the country in which he (or she) was 'whelped'. Wolf-lore was not prevalent in Ireland but Stoker taps into a vein of the collective unconscious and paints a skilful picture to stimulate the reader's imagination. In the opening chapter of *Dracula*, as Jonathon Harker gets nearer to the castle, the scene is set by the symbolic passing from civilisation into the wild:

> ... The keen wind still carried the howling of the dogs, though this grew fainter as we went on our way. The baying of the wolves sounded nearer and near, as though they were closing round us from every side ... I could not see any cause for it, for the howling of the wolves had ceased altogether; but just then the moon sailing through the black clouds, appeared behind the jagged crest of beetling, pine clad rock, and by its

light I saw around us a ring of wolves, with white teeth and lolling red tongues, with long, sinewy limbs and shaggy hair. They were a hundred times more terrible in the grim silence which held them than even when they howled …

Dracula has the ability to manifest as a wolf and this chilling start to Harker's adventure loses none of its impact with the knowing that he emerges from this encounter unscathed. Nevertheless, the image of the wolf is one of the most chilling of Nature's creations, not just because of its immense strength and killing ability, but because of its intelligence and high cunning. To quote again from Madame Gerard:

Every winter here brings fresh proof of the boldness and cunning of these terrible animals, whose attacks on flocks and farms are often conducted with a skill which would do honour to a human intellect. Sometimes a whole village is kept in trepidation for weeks together by some particularly audacious lead of a flock [sic] of wolves, to whom the peasants not unnaturally attribute a more than animal nature …

One of the briefest, but most suggestive episodes in *Dracula* is where a mother comes up from the village to the castle and demands the Count return her child. Her entreaties are met by his summoning of the wolves and "a pack of them poured, like a pent-up dam when liberated, through the wide entrance into the courtyard. There was no cry from the woman, and the howling of the wolves was but short. Before long they streamed away singly licking their lips." It demonstrates how little this un-dead aristocrat cared about his peasantry – which in my experience has always been a dangerous attitude since one learns very early in Life to fear the mob!

Because of these graphic descriptions, wolves have become firmly imprinted in the collective unconscious and as Stefan

Buczacki (obviously himself having East European roots) observes in *Fauna Britannica*:

> To my mind, one of the greatest differences between life in Britain today and a thousand years ago is not the absence of sanitation, transport or medicine, but the deeply entrenched fear of knowing that you were sharing the countryside with the Wolf. To know that you might encounter a Wolf just beyond your village and almost anywhere you walked in the still-vast native forests would surely colour your life and activities to an unimaginable degree.

Possibly one of the world's most fearsome and respected of animals, and although a fear of wolves is prevalent in most human society, attacks on humans are unusual. The wolf's own roots, however, dig deep and appear as a common motif in mythology and folklore throughout Eurasia and North America, which also corresponds to the animal's original natural habitat. The howling of wolves across untamed countryside has an eerie, terrifying and yet magical sound. As Jack London wrote in *The Call of the Wild*: "From the forest came the call (or one note of it, for the call was many-noted), distinct and definite as never before – a long-drawn howl, like, yet unlike, any noise made by husky dog ..."

The wolf is not just a formidable creature in its natural habitat, ironically it is also synonymous with courage and daring in man – look at how extensively the wolf has been used in heraldry to support this claim. Widely used in many forms during the Middle Ages, and although commonly reviled as a livestock predator and alleged man-eater, the wolf was also considered a noble and courageous animal in the chase; frequently appearing on the Arms of numerous noble European families. In many instances it was probably the historical equivalent of the modern concave-chested, pimply youth sporting a T-shirt exclaiming

'Hail Satan!' But I digress ...

The *Concise Encyclopaedia of Heraldry* demonstrates that this wolf-obsession in heraldry can be traced back to the dawn of history, before writing, when pictorial representations were used to identify individuals, families, clans and tribes. Early on, it took its place as an integral part of warfare; by the Middle Ages it had become a complex system of fabulous coloured images since in the heat of armour-clad combat, it was a vital means of distinguishing friend from foe.

> Wolves naturally play a big part. They are shown 'rampant' (erect on its hind legs), 'passant'(walking past in profile), 'courant' (running), 'vorant (devouring prey), 'ravisant' (carrying it off), and in many other positions; while their heads are favourite charges. It is significant that the ravisant wolf is often seen on Spanish shields. Wolves are borne as warlike or sporting symbols, but quite often as punning allusion to the wearers ...

Wolves appeared frequently in English heraldry: an early shield bearing two wolf heads was attributed to the Earl of Chester, circa 1070, while 'two wolf heads erased azure' were later used on the Arms of subsequent Earls. Edward IV (1442–83) used a white wolf for one of his badges, along with a white lion, denoting his descent from the House of Mortimer. The wolf or its head is often used for canting on names such as Videlou, de Lou (both recorded in the anonymous Great Roll of 1308–14); Lupus (in the reign of Edward III; Wolferston (in the *Henry VI Roll,* circa 1422–61), Wolseley, Lovett, Low, Lovell, Lupton and of course Wolfe, Wolfton and Wolverton. The wolf is also featured in the heraldry of continental nations, particularly those from Eastern Europe. In German heraldry the town of Passau (Bavaria) bears a red wolf rampant on a white shield. In Saxony, a black wolf rampant on a yellow shield features on the crest of von

Wolfersdorf family. A green wolf grasping a dead swan in its jaws on a yellow shield is depicted on the crest and Arms of the Counts von Brandenstein-Zeppelin.

In more modern times, the coat of arms of the secular separatists in Chechnya bore the wolf, because the wolf (*borz*) was the Chechen nation's national embodiment and is still used by the secular government in exile. In addition, many other insignia of the Chechen nation (of all three governments) use the wolf as a heraldic symbol. Not only is it the national animal, but the Chechen people are symbolically said to be variously related to wolves (in an either symbolic or joking manner), and there are legends of their ancestors being raised by a 'wolf mother'. Characteristics of the wolf are also frequently compared to the Chechen people in a poetic sense, including the most famous line that members of the Chechen nation are 'free and equal like wolves'.

It appears that every nobleman in Christendom wanted to be identified with the daring and courage of the wolf – and then promptly hunted it to extinction. It is in European folklore, however that this noble animal comes into its own; where the wolf is viewed with fearsome awe and represented as much more dangerous to man than it actually is. Because wolves were seen on the battlefields feeding on the slain, they were transformed by imagination into sinister supernatural creatures. While during times of famine or severe weather conditions, wolves would move closer to human dwellings to feed on fallen stock and afflicted humans. According to *Man, Myth & Magic:*

Northern [European] peoples generally seem to have viewed the wolf with a fear and hate bordering on hysteria – the kind usually reserved for the worst supernatural monsters ... But there is more to the fear of the wolf than a mere antipathy to a beast of prey. The wolf seems to be regarded by Europeans as somehow in itself demonic. Wolves are semi-nocturnal, usually greyish in colour, and move in an almost ghostly silence. They have slanting eyes that glow yellow-green in the moonlight, red in reflected firelight. And their chilling, banshee-like howl completes the eerie picture.

And this view is supported by scientist Stephen Budiansky (*The Truth About Dogs*), who observed that even when socialised with humans from puppyhood, wolves retain a high, and dangerous degree of unpredictability. Also, that while it is true that there are extremely few if any reliable accounts of other than rabid wolves attacking and injuring humans in the wild, this is mainly because wolves in the wild are wary and generally maintain a substantial distance from humans.

But wolves that are raised in captivity lose some their fear of approaching humans – and with proximity comes trouble. Erik Zimen, a German biologist who carried out extensive behavioural studies of wolves, both in captivity and in the wild, found that captive wolves who had the closest relationships with humans were by far the most dangerous and unpredictable.

In other words, even semi-tame, the wolf unsettles humans on some deep atavistic level that is buried deep within the collective unconscious where it is closely associated with all 'children of the night'. Atavism refers to the re-emergence of the ancestral characteristics of what may be after many generations, and the implication is nearly always of something unwholesome and frightening – an idea that has been used in many horror stories – of things that come from the time of creatures half-man and half-beast. The twilight world of the vampire.

The word atavism is derived from the Latin *atavus*, which generally speaking means 'ancestor' and is often used to refer to a cultural return of old, more primitive tendencies. 'Resurgent atavism' is a popular reference to the belief that people in contemporary society are beginning to revert to attitudes and actions that are throwbacks to a former time. The neo-pagan sub-culture falls into this category in embracing spiritual movements inspired by the pagan beliefs of centuries past, with modern pagans (particularly shamanic) often adopting the wolf as a clan totem or power animal. A few of them, as we shall see, even adopt the lifestyle of the vampire whilst still living!

The wolf is a racial-memory from the dark side of the psyche, evoking feelings, patterns of thought, and fragments of experience that have been transmitted from generation to generation in all humans. *This* is what Carl Jung labelled the 'collective unconscious', and Sigmund Freud call 'archaic remnants' – mental forms or images whose presence cannot be explained by anything in an individual's own life or background. No doubt the attitude towards vampires may also come from this racial-memory if our ancestral roots dig deep into the time when we were a fact of life and not merely entertaining bedtime reading.

Wolves, of course, were synonymous with vampires in Europe, and in the Winter 1995 issue of *Udolpho* magazine, Derek Brockis introduced the readership to the fascinating legend of La Bête with the words, "The French have kept one of the world's best monster mysteries to themselves for over two hundred years: who was 'La Bête du Gévaudan' who prowled the Auvergne, tore people to pieces, drank their blood, and seemed invulnerable to bullets?" And of this supernatural canine Robert Louis Stevenson once wrote: "If all wolves had been this wolf they would have changed the history of man."

Despite being relatively unknown outside France, the kills accredited to La Bête are meticulously chronicled, with names, dates and injuries of the victims recorded in detail for almost every murder. In fact there was no village in Gévaudan whose parish registers did not contain the sinister recording: "Death certificate of the body of .... eaten partially by the ferocious

Beast." She was described as wolf-like but not a wolf: she often attacked in an upright position, partially devouring the victims unless disturbed, often crushing heads, eating entrails and draining their blood.

> While she prowled, inhabitants of farms and villages suffered seriously from lack of sleep; every noise at night raised the households in panic, so tense were their nerves. When woken up, they were too terrified to drag away the clumsy wooden shutters and look out, because those who did often found themselves staring straight into La Bête's eyes, with no glass between them and her, and her claws on the windowsill. They were lucky that unlike Jack the Ripper and the Vampire of Dusseldorf, she never entered houses.
>
> Derek Brockis, *The Return of La Bête*

Eventually three very big wolves were killed, one of which was sent to Paris and presented to Louis XV but the killings went on for a further two years; in 1767 a certain Jean Chastel killed a deformed wolf accepted by some as La Bête but this was far from proven, since there had been so many reports of the creature's demise. The official 'Bête du Gévaudan' website shows that she killed or wounded 240 people, mostly women and children during a five-year period, and although whole regiments of soldiers hunted her, she was never caught, killed, or fully explained. In 2006, Derek Brockis finally tracked down a French edition of Abbe Pierre Pourchier's *Bête du Gévaudan* (1889) and translated it into English in order to share the mystery of La Bête with the world.

Descriptions of *La Bête* are the same for many sightings and for other beasts recorded in this region of France in the centuries before and after her most famous killing spree. "The prints and engravings show her almost universally as a rakish, elegant creature – after all, she was French – often in action on two legs," wrote Derek Brockis. "She was last seen strolling along at Sarlat, a prehistoric cave area just outside Gévaudan, on 4th August 1767 … after that she vanished into the mists of history."

The question of who or what *La Bête* was remains a mystery but my suggestion would be that she was another creature from the racial memory – hence the rather affectionate position she retains in French folklore. Similarly in Normandy, tradition tells of other fantastic beings known as *lupins* or *lubins*, depicted in the famous picture, *Les Lupins*, by Maurice Sand, for the compilation of French folklore by George Sand, called *Legendes Rustiques*, published in 1858.

> They pass the night chattering together and twattling in an unknown tongue. They take their stand by the walls of country cemeteries, and howl dismally at the moon. Timorous and fearful of man they will flee away scared at a footstep or distant voice. In some districts, however, they are fierce and of the werewolf race, since they are said to scratch up the graves with their hands, and gnaw the poor dead bones.

The French suffered terribly from wolves in the past, which explains the abundance of werewolf tales from the country. *Loup-garou*, the French word for werewolf, referred to a person who turns into a wolf at night and terrorizes the surrounding countryside, killing people and livestock, and devouring their flesh. In French folklore, which is rich in such creatures, he can be cured if three drops of blood are taken from him, or if he is made to bleed while in wolf-form.

In many parts of France, but more especially in Brittany, *Le Meneur des Loups* is a wizard who meets and sits with the werewolves around a fire kindled in the heart of the forest and then leads the howling pack on their nocturnal chase. "Gathering the werewolves around him, he gives them directions, telling them what farms or towns are ill-guarded that night, what flocks, what herds, are negligently kept, which path the lonely wayfarer setting out from the inn is taking ..." (*The Werewolf*, Montague Summers)

Although the myth of the werewolf is of long standing, the first one I ever came face to face with was the elaborately made up Lon Chaney Jr in the film *The Wolf Man*!

The werewolf itself is often described as being first cousin to the vampire (an ancestry that I hotly dispute!) and in *Transylvania Superstitions*, Madame Gerard describes it as

the long-exploded werewolf of the Germans is here to be found, lingering yet under the name of the *prikolitsch*. Sometimes it is a dog instead of a wolf, whose form a man has taken either voluntarily, or as a penance for his sins ... We do not require to go far for the explanation of the extraordinary tenacity of life of the werewolf legend in a country like Transylvania, where real wolves still abound [1885] ... and one may safely prophesy that so long as the real wolf continues to haunt the Transylvania forests, so long will his spectre brother survive in the minds of the inhabitants.

Adam Douglas in his *The Beast Within: A History of the Werewolf*, however, has tracked doggedly down the evolution of the myth of the werewolf from pre-history up to the present day. He suggests that folklore, by "mythologizing medical conditions such as congenital porphyria and melancholic lycanthropia, helped to give rise to the werewolf legends that date back to the Middle Ages. By the time of the Renaissance, however, incidences of lycanthropy had reached epidemic proportions, and like the witchcraft trials, hunters were employed to rid Europe of this 'diabolical plague'." And from *Man, Myth & Magic*:

In legend, the werewolf is a living person who has the magical power to change his or her shape. In its bestial form it is a terroriser, a killer, an eater of human flesh. These two elements – metamorphosis and murder – form the basis, and much of the substance, of the legend. But the werewolf's family tree is ancient, vast, and has many spreading branches. Some branches lead to the realm of revenants (those who have returned from the dead), where ghosts and vampires walk; other lead to evil sorcery, witchcraft and diabolism.

The myth of the man turning himself into a ravening beast has persisted down through the ages, but I would not embrace one as a 'first cousin'. To be brutally frank, the werewolf has little history that doesn't ride on the reputation of the vampire. For example, in medieval Europe, the corpses of those executed as werewolves were cremated rather than buried in order to prevent them from being resurrected as vampires; while in my homeland of Greece, prior to the end of the 19th century, the belief was that the corpses of werewolves, if not destroyed, would return to life as vampires in the form of wolves that prowled battlefields, drinking the blood of dying soldiers. In similar vein, in rural areas of Germany, Poland and Northern France, it was often believed that people who died in mortal sin came back to life as blood-drinking wolves, although the creature was a *living* being rather than one of the un-dead.

In *The Werewolf Delusion*, Ian Woodward goes on to explain that these 'vampiric werewolves' would return to their human corpse form at daylight. "They were dealt with by decapitation with a spade and exorcism by the parish priest. The head would then be thrown into a stream, where the weight of its sins was thought to weigh it down. Sometimes, the same methods used to dispose of ordinary vampires would be used." The vampire was also linked to the werewolf in East European countries, particularly Bulgaria, Serbia and Slovenia; in Serbia, the werewolf and vampire are known collectively as one creature; *Vulkodlak* while in Hungarian and Balkan mythology, many werewolves were said to be 'vampiric witches' who became wolves in order to suck the blood of men born under the full moon in order to preserve their health. 'Tis no wonder than confusion reigns!

The familiar werewolf phenomena is frequently the subject of the modern fantasy or horror genre, and the concept that they can only be destroyed by silver bullets or some other silver weapon derives from 20th-century fiction. Contemporary werewolf fiction almost exclusively involves lycanthropy being either a hereditary condition, or being transmitted like an infectious disease by the bite of another werewolf. In medieval Europe the traditional methods for curing a victim were medicinally (using wolfsbane), surgically or by exorcism, although unlike vampires they are not generally to be harmed by religious artefacts such as crucifixes and holy water. According to Adam Douglas, however, no werewolf was safe from Henri Boguet, "whose role in the werewolf persecutions was the equivalent of Matthew Hopkins, the Witch-Finder General" and even though there were guidelines of how to investigate alleged cases "at the height of the werewolf hysteria it was usual to burn first and ask questions later."

Unlike the vampire, there were no literary classics to draw upon for the werewolf, and despite the explosion of short stories and novels in the 20th century, including Guy Endore's cult-classic *The Werewolf in Paris* in 1933 (that was later adapted for film as *The Curse of the Werewolf* in 1961 for Hammer), the werewolf never really attained cult status. *Films of Science Fiction and Fantasy* by B Searles points out that the first to use an anthropomorphic werewolf was *Werewolf of London* in 1935, with the main character as a "dapper London scientist who retains some of his style and most of his human features after his transformation, as lead actor Henry Hull was unwilling to spend long hours being made up ... Universal Studios drew on a Balkan tale of a plant associated with lycanthropy as there was no literary work to draw upon, unlike the case with vampires."

A more empathic portrayal was that of Lon Chaney Jr's tragic character, Larry Talbot in *The Wolf Man* (1941), and similar in approach to *Varney, the Vampire,* in that the reluctant 'victim' was a creature of circumstance rather than evil. With more elaborate makeup the film catapulted the werewolf into public consciousness, although sympathetic portrayals were few – "such as the comedic but tortured protagonist David Naughton in *An American Werewolf in London,* and a less anguished and more confident and charismatic Jack Nicholson in the 1994 film *Wolf,*" observes Brad Steiger in *The Werewolf Book: The Encyclopaedia of Shapeshifting Beings.*

Rachel Hawthorne's *Dark Guardian* novels examine a secret society of werewolves who live peacefully alongside normal humans, are able to initiate the change at will to protect their kind, and generally retain control of themselves when trans-formed. Other werewolves are decidedly more malevolent, such as those in the novel *The Howling* and its subsequent sequels and film adaptations. The form a werewolf assumes was generally anthropomorphic in early films such as *The Wolf Man* and *Werewolf of London,* but morphed into a much larger and more terrifying wolf in later films according to *Horror Movies: An Illustrated Survey.*

Cinematic werewolves are often depicted as immune to damage caused by ordinary weapons, being vulnerable only to silver objects, as in silver-tipped cane, bullet or blade; this attribute was first adopted cinematically in *The Wolf Man.* According to Brad Steiger, this negative reaction to silver is sometimes so strong that the mere touch of the metal on a werewolf's skin will cause burns. In fiction, the power of the werewolf often extends to human form, such as invulnerability to conventional injury due to their healing factor, super-human speed and strength and falling on their feet from high falls. Also aggressiveness and animalistic urges may be intensified and harder to control (hunger, sexual arousal). Usually in these cases the abilities are diminished in human form.

In other fiction it can be cured by medicine men or antidotes. Fantastic literature sometimes includes the painful element to the change, but often does not. For example, J. K. Rowling maintains the painful transition between forms while Charles de Lint, Terry Pratchett, Fritz Leiber, and myriad others reach back to the non-painful medieval literary sources. Poul Anderson presents a modernised American werewolf, in complete control of himself and free of the traditional taints in *Operation Chaos*, but uses a far more traditional (though not unsympathetic) female werewolf in his *Three Hearts and Three Lions*.

According to Douglas Hill, however, writing in *Man, Myth & Magic*, the werewolf is just as sexual a figure as the vampire, but "lacks the sado-erotic subtlety. Werewolves are crude rapists and murderers, with a few ghoulish or cannibalistic overtones and belong to the realm of sado-masochistic fantasies." Not the sort of chap one would encourage in one's circle of friends and acquaintances, I fear.

In most European cultures, that other 'child of the night' the bat has also been long associated with vampires, witchcraft and the powers of darkness, although the vampire bat often featured in films is a native species of the New World, living in arid to humid, tropical and sub-tropical areas – and therefore plays no part in European folklore. In vampire films, however, a large bat is often seen hovering outside a potential victim's bedroom window, suggesting that the vampire can either transform itself into a bat, or that the creature acts as an infernal messenger.

The bat's physical characteristics and its apparently supernatural ability to hunt its prey in total darkness have been largely responsible for the frightening reputation it has acquired over the ages as a creature of occult power – similar to those of the owl. It was an established principle in medieval times that the Devil often assumed the shape of a bat, and so the animal was only one step away from being identified with the vampire. When Jonathan Harker describes the Count "begin to crawl down the castle wall over that dreadful abyss, face down, with his cloak spreading out around him like great wings," we instantly form the picture in our mind's eye of a gigantic bat.

And finally, for aficionados of the vampire genre 'The Children of the Night Award' is also an annual prize given by the Dracula Society for the best piece of literature published in the Gothic (including horror and supernatural) genre for the previous year. One might be tempted to enter one's own literary offering ...

Chapter Seven

Film and Fakelore

Surprisingly enough, Polidori's *The Vampyre* has never made it onto the silver screen, but I must confess that I am arrogant enough to be concerned over who would be chosen to play my part. I would have gone for a young David Bowie if he hadn't already done *The Hunger*, and I am certainly impressed by the versatile talents of Johnny Depp, who remains so remarkably young looking for his age that one is almost tempted to study *his* antecedents more closely!

Like all elements of 'the arts' the horror genre comes and goes in cycles, waiting for a new generation to discover its spine-tingling delights. *Dracula* is as popular now as when it was first written and millions of people worldwide are familiar with the film versions, if not actually having read the novel. Late night television has brought us face to face with the most critically acclaimed classic filmed versions such *Nosferatu*, made with Max Schreck (1922), *Dracula* with Bela Lugosi (1931) and *Horror of Dracula* with Christopher Lee (1958).

Although not the best looking of the bunch, Count Orlok's rodent-like features were the German director's idea of what a real vampire would look like – cadaverous, skeletal and withered. In 1921, almost a quarter of a century after the stage play, *Dracula*, or *the Un-dead*, F. W. Murnau, a young German film director, decided to make the first horror film about Stoker's character. Although Murnau gave full credit on the screen to the author, he had failed to obtain permission to use it and, as a result, he was forced to change the setting from Transylvania to the Baltic, and added his own erotic ending.

This silent film, entitled *Nosferatu*, was released by Prana Films in Berlin in 1922 and although Stoker had since died, his widow Florence sued Murnau, won the case and his film company went out of business. The court ordered the negative and prints of *Nosferatu* to be destroyed but fortunately for vampire film buffs, this did not happen and it opened in London in 1928. Since then, it has continued to be shown to appreciative audiences of the arts cinema across the world – *despite* the unappealing appearance of Max Schreck's Orlok. Needless to say, there were many deviations from the original novel, such as name changes, the omission of secondary characters and using a different location – all of which set the time-honoured trend for dramatising novels for the silver screen; and it is said that the television movie of *Salem's Lot* based its leading vampire's appearance on Count Orlock.

As the stage versions of *Dracula* were a huge success in both the UK and the USA, film director Tod Browning bought the film rights to the Deane-Balderston version for Universal Pictures in 1930. Bela Lugosi, the now famous stage Dracula, was hired to play the lead, which was released on 14th February 1931. A natural choice for the role, Lugosi was at least a native Hungarian and his "deep, thick accent and slow manner of speaking, his aquiline nose, high cheek bones and six-foot frame all seemed perfect attributes for the part. The eerie effect of his almond-shaped, crystal-blue eyes was heightened in the film by focusing light on them through two small holes in a piece of cardboard." (*Hollywood Gothic*) The film became Universal's biggest box-office draw for 1931.

There followed a long line of horror films in which Lugosi starred, including *Dracula's Daughter* (1936) and he toured in the role of Dracula both in the UK and USA, but unfortunately he was addicted to drugs, having been receiving regular medication for sciatic neuritis, and by 1955 was in an institution. In August 1956, Bela Lugoi, the vampire king, the living embodiment of Dracula, died at 73 years of age of a heart attack … and in accordance with his family's request, was buried in a black Dracula cloak lined with red satin in the Holy Cross Cemetery in Culver City. The cape he actually wore in the 1931 film of *Dracula* remains the property of Universal Studios.

And the Lugosi legacy lived on ... in Andy Warhol's 1963 silkscreen – *The Kiss* – which depicts the Count about to sink his fangs into the neck of Mina Harker, played by Helen Chandler in the film, sold as a print copy for $798,000 at Christie's in 2000. A single record by English rock band, Bauhaus – *Bela Lugosi's Dead* – was released in August 1979 and is often considered to be the first Gothic rock recording. The song can be heard at the start of the soundtrack for the 1983 vampire film, *The Hunger*.

By 1958, however, there was a new king to take the crown of whom I fully approved. Director Terence Fisher cast Christopher Lee for a Hammer Films version of *Dracula* based wholly on Stoker's story line. Lee was tall and lean, with an aristocratic bearing and deep, strong voice that was deadly attractive to women, and an erotic element of the 'lady killer' was introduced into the genre that Lugosi could never inspire, since he often gave the impression of a gigolo and not to be taken seriously as a sex symbol. The new *Dracula* opened in May 1958 in London and New York, and in less than two years had made eight times its original cost.

Christopher Lee has since made the role of the Count his own, but was less than happy with subsequent Hammer films: *Dracula: Prince of Darkness* (1965), *Dracula Has Risen From The Grave* (1968), *Taste The Blood of Dracula* (1969), and *Scars of Dracula* (1970), but they were commercially successful and are now also considered classics of the genre. He was fortunate that following the close of the Hammer studios, he did not suffer too much from typecasting and has since appeared in such cinema greats such as *The Wicker Man* (1973), *Star Wars* (2002), *The Lord of the Rings* (2001–2003) and *The Hobbit* trilogy (2012–2014).

As a result of all this cinematic activity, the vampire is considered to be one of the pre-eminent fictional characters of the cult-classic horror film, and provided rich pickings for both the movie and gaming industries. In fact, Dracula is a major character in more films than any other but Sherlock Holmes, and many early vampire films were either based on the novel of *Dracula* or closely derived from it. Eventually screenwriters were forced to created different scenarios that were often ludicrous to the point of imbecility when compared to the classic sources.

A welcome relief came in Roman Polanski's black comedy, *Dance of the Vampires* (1967 – or *The Fearless Vampire Killers*) that featured the most unlikely of vampire hunters – old and withered Professor Abronsius and his assistant, bumbling and introverted Alfred. They are on the trail of Count von Krolock, the local vampire with a penchant for abducting village maidens to provide the buffet at the castle's annual vampiric knees-up. The ball sequence provides another of those cinematic 'moments' in the film's climactic *danse macabre* minuet, where the Professor and Alfred join the dancers only to find, on facing a large mirror at the end of the promenade, that they are alone in the ballroom. Ivan Butler writing in *The Cinema of Roman Polanski* quoted the film's cinematographer Dougles Slocombe as saying:

I think he [Polanski] put more of himself into *Dance of the Vampires* than into another film. It brought to light the fairy-tale interest that he has. One was conscious all along when making the picture of a Central European background to the story. Very few of the crew could see anything in it – they thought it old-fashioned nonsense. But I could see this background ... I have a French background myself, and could sense the Central European atmosphere that surrounds it. The figure of Alfred is very much like Roman himself – a slight figure, young and a little defenceless – a touch of Kafka. It is very much a personal statement of his own humour. He used to chuckle all the way through.

On a more serious note, *In Search of Dracula* was produced in 1972 by Aspekt Films and the authors of the book of the same name, Raymond McNally and Radu Florescu, served as historical consultants.

> This film is an entertaining documentary about the real Dracula and Transylvania folklore, shot on location in present-day Romania. It is the first film to deal with both the fictional vampire Count Dracula and the genuinely historical Vlad the Impaler. Clips from famous *Dracula* films are interwoven with scenes from Transylvanian folklore about vampires. Christopher Lee is the narrator, and appeared in native costume.

The legend of the vampire was firmly cemented in the film industry when Dracula was reincarnated for subsequent movies, proving to be almost indestructible, despite the innovative and more spectacular ways of killing him off at the end of each new incarnation. By the 1970s, vampires in films had diversified with works such as the gory *Count Yorga, Vampire* (1970 – also known as *The Loves of Count Iorga*) followed by the sequel, *The Return of Count Yorga*, starring Robert Quarry. The actor later played another vampire, Khorda, in *The Deathmaster* (1973) that is often confused with the Yorga films, but since few people remember them, this confusion hardly muddies the waters of the fast running stream.

The first to tackle *Carmilla* was French filmmaker, Roger Vadim (1960), famed for his sexually explicit movies, he directed *Blood and Roses* (*Et Mourir De Plaisir*), shifting the locale from 19th century Styria to 20th century Italy. The vampire manifests following a masquerade ball, when a firework display accidentally explodes some lost WWII munitions with all its accompanying pyrotechnics, disturbing an ancestral catacomb. The modern Carmilla, wearing a copy of the dress of her legendary vampire ancestor wanders into the ruins, where the tomb of the ancestor slowly opens ... Unfortunately, the English version of the film omits important parts of the original French script where the doctor's narrative sets the ball rolling (as it does in the novella) and the discussions of vampire legends by the servant's children to help set the scene.

The next time *Carmilla* was adapted for film was ten years later when several films featured female vampire antagonists such as Hammer Horror's *The Vampire Lovers* (1970) based on Sheridan Le Fanu's original novella, with the plotline revolving around a central seductive vampire character played by the smouldering Ingrid Pitt. The film was part of the so-called *Karnstein Trilogy* – the others being *Lust For a Vampire* (1971) and *Twins of Evil* (1972) – and were considered somewhat daring for the time in explicitly depicting lesbian themes. The dramatic end to *The Vampire Lovers* occurs when Carmilla is decapitated and her portrait on the wall decays to reveal a fanged skeleton instead of a beautiful young woman, *a la Dorian Grey.*

Ingrid Pitt also starred in the title role of *Countess Dracula* (1971), another Hammer horror film based on the real-life Elizabeth Bathory. The plot, however, is so convoluted that it bears little resemblance to historical accuracy and concentrates on virgin and blood sacrifices in lieu of a sensible narrative. *The Hammer Story: The Authorised History of Hammer Films* records that the film's "distinctly anaemic blood-lettings fail to lift a rather tiresome tale of court intrigue," – even the popular actress being unable to lift it out of the mundane.

Blacula (1972) concerns an 18th-century African prince, who is turned into a vampire by Dracula, and locked inside a coffin by the Count after a party at his Transylvanian castle. Two hundred years later the prince is released from his coffin and begins killing the residents of modern-day Los Angles. His first two victims are the interior designers who have brought the coffin from Europe to the USA – incongruously, no one had ever thought to look inside the coffin for all those years! The vampire is finally despatched by sunlight rotting his flesh: there was a sequel in 1973 – *Scream, Blacula, Scream* – which is hardly worth a mention.

Despite its distinguished cast, *Incense for the Damned* (also released as *Bloodsuckers*) is a 1970 British horror film that takes the brilliant and witty novel, *Doctors Wear Scarlet* by Simon Raven, and turns it into incomprehensible gibberish. The plot centres on a young student who has disappeared in Greece and when his friends search for him they discover a series of murders have been committed. They eventually discover him under thrall to a beautiful vampire, Chriseis, whose blood-sucking methods include S&M sex. Having killed her, the party returns to England, not realising that their friend has become a vampire – it is a toss-up whether the soporific effect of the film is due to the wacky-baccy era or sheer boredom.

Jack Palance starred in a television adaptation of *Dracula* (1973) with a slight twist to the plot, in that Count believes Lucy Westenra to be his reincarnated lost love. With a distinctive Slavic cast to his features, Ukranian-bred Palance was an ideal *Dracula* – three years before he played the part, comic book artist, Gene Colan, had based his interpretation of the Count for his Marvel series *The Tomb of Dracula: Lord of the Vampires* on the actor, saying, "He had that cadaverous look, a serpentine look on his face. I knew that Jack Palance would do the perfect Dracula." An accomplished method actor, Palance's roar of rage and pain on discovering that Lucy has died a second time by being despatched with a wooden stake through her heart, is another of those 'moments' of cinematic history. This Dracula's end comes when, weakened by sunlight streaming through the curtainless windows, Van Helsing pierces his heart with a long spear. The camera focuses on a portrait of the living Dracula, with a Lucy lookalike in the background.

The vampire myth also appealed to the pornography market and a French-Belgian film, *Female Vampire* (originally made as

The Bare Breasted Countess: 1973) features a vampire who has sex with both male and female victims. Described as 'an unusual variation of the vampire myth', the vampires performs oral sex on her victims until they die, draining them of their sexual fluids. Three versions of the film were shot – straight horror, horror mixed with sex, and the hard-core pornography version, all of which no doubt brought tears to the eyes of the male viewers.

The Tomb of Dracula was a comic book 70-issue series published by Marvel Comics (1972–1979) and featured a group of vampire hunters who were constantly at odds with Dracula or some other supernatural menace. Marvel had already introduced *Morbius, the Living Vampire* but wanted to introduce a regular vampire title to their new line of horror books, and went for Dracula as a familiar character and because Stoker's "creation and secondary characters were by that time in the public domain," i.e. out of copyright, according to Peter Sanderson in *Marvel Chronicle: A Year by Year History*. It became the most successful comic book series to feature a villain as its title character. The series ended with the death of the main characters but several years later the 'vampire lord' was revived and has continued to stalk the corridors of pulp fiction ever since.

Count Dracula was a British television adaptation (1977) that remained faithful to Stoker's original novel, and although the attractive, urbane and seductive Louis Jourdan might not find favour with the purists, the critics were generally positive. Film historian, Stuart Galbraith considered it to be one of the best-ever adaptations of the original novel; while film critic Steve Calvert agreed, saying that few actors had ever played the role of Van Helsing as convincingly as Frank Findlay. He also felt that Jack Shepherd's on-screen embodiment of 'the fly-munching Renfield' was the best there'd ever been and that Jourdan's performance "… exudes a quieter kind of evil. A calculating, educated evil with a confidence and purpose of its own." Unfortunately, in true cinema scriptwriting tradition, Jourdan was despatched by

Professor Van Helsing using a stake through the heart, rather than the fictional cutting of Dracula's throat with Jonathan Harker's *kukri*, and stabbed through the heart with Quincey Morris's Bowie knife.

There was a return to a Nosferatu-like vampire in the American television mini-series adaptation of Stephen King's novel, *Salem's Lot* (1979), where a writer returns to his hometown to discover that his neighbours are turning into vampires with depressing regularity. The story combines elements of both the vampire and the haunted house sub-genre, although several characters, sub-plots and violence from the original story were deleted from the screenplay. *Salem's Lot* is recognised in the film world as having a significant influence on the later vampire genre, inspiring the horror vampire classic *Fright Night* (1985), the scenes of vampire boys floating outside windows in *The Lost Boys* (1987) and the television hit-series *Buffy, the Vampire Slayer.*

1979 also saw a German remake of Nosferatu as *Nosferatu the Vampyre* (or *Nosferatu: Phantom of the Night*) with Klaus Kinski in the title role; it was conceived as a stylish remake of the 1922 original and achieved a certain amount of commercial success. In *Nosferatu The Vampyre*, David Keyes observes that "Herzog's production maintained an element of horror, with numerous deaths and a grim atmosphere, but it features a more expanded plot than many *Dracula* productions, with a greater emphasis of the vampire's tragic loneliness. Dracula is still a ghastly figure, but with a greater sense of pathos; weary, unloved and doomed to immortality." Oh dear!

Occasionally, a film would show the vampire as protagonist, such as *The Hunger* (1983) that was loosely based on the Whitley Strieber novel of the same name and starring Catherine Deneuve and David Bowie. These modern day vampires live in an elegant townhouse in New York, posing as a wealthy couple who teach classical music; periodically they feed on human victims as vampires. Camille Paglia (*Sexual Personae: Art and Decadence from*

Nefertiti to Emily Dickinson) wrote that *The Hunger* came close to being a masterpiece of a "classy genre of vampire film, but that it was ruined by horrendous errors, as when the regal Catherine Deneuve is made to crawl around on all fours, slavering over cut throats." Despite its mixed reception, the film has found a cult following that "responded to its dark, glamorous atmosphere" and inspired a short-lived television series of the same name.

Nevertheless, it must be Francis Ford Coppola's all-star production of *Bram Stoker's Dracula* (1992) with Gary Oldman and Winona Ryder that gets the prize for 'fantasy egg-laying' – or as Duncan Barford's review in *Udolpho* magazine echoed the thoughts of many a true vampire lover:

> … There are some fine cinematic special effects in the film, yet, as a whole, it flounders and fluffs. In lacks pace and narrative tension, which makes its appropriation of the original author's name in the title seem doubly arrogant. Bram Stoker's 1897 novel is a well crafted and executed Gothic Masterpiece. It is presumptuous of Coppola to suggest that his film is what Stoker himself intended, and to assert that there is in fact any need for Stoker to be 'translated' into film. The original *Dracula* is already there, waiting to be read … It's enough to make any self-respecting, traditionalist vampire heartily sick. And it's a million miles away from the sumptuous Gothic depiction of lust and disease in Bram Stoker's original.

One suspects that the 15th-century opening and closing sequences (which do not remotely resemble anything in the narrative of Bram Stoker's *Dracula*) provided the opportunity for lavish special effects. Coupled with Gary Oldman's ridiculous, pantomime-dame pompadour the whole left aficionados reeling with horror at the blatant desecration of a much-loved novel.

Surprisingly, it is the 'small screen' that has provided the constant life's blood for the vampire. The pilot for the Dan Curtis

1973–4 television series *Kolchak: The Night Stalker* revolved around reporter Carl Kolchak hunting a vampire on the Las Vegas strip. The series was preceded by two television movies, *The Night Stalker* (1971) and *The Night Strangler* (1973), a serial killer who strangled his victims and used their blood to keep himself alive for over a century. Once the television movie and its sequel had gone out on air, the original (previously unpublished) novel by Jeff Rice was brought out by Pocket Books as a mass-market paperback to tie in with the series, and *The Night Stalker* was published in 1974.

Later films showed more diversity of imagination in the plotline, with some focusing on the vampire-hunter, such as Blade in the Marvel Comics' fantasy *Blade* films (1998). The original comic character was created in 1973 but the film version was updated for the 1990s, and the comic characters were subsequently modified to match. The Afro-American vampire-superhero is played by Wesley Snipes, whose mother was bitten by a vampire (*Blacula*!?) before he was born. The film was highly popular and grossed $131.2 million at the box office worldwide – and was followed by two sequels, *Blade II* and *Blade: Trinity*.

Interview with the Vampire, the first of *The Vampire Chronicles* (1994) is based on the novel by Anne Rice, beginning with Louis's (Brad Pitt) transformation into a vampire by Lestat (Tom Cruise) in 1791 Louisiana. As in the novel, the narrative is framed by a present day interview, in which Louis tells his story to a reporter. Antonio Banderas, as the dark brooding Armand, introduces the New World vampires to the Old World traditions of Théâtre des Vampires, which is perhaps the most dramatic and atmospheric element in the story. Ironically, the child-vampire Claudia is around 12 years old in the film, but in the original novel she "was only five at most" and this is the most chilling aspect of the book that is missing from the film version. Perhaps the filmmakers considered this be bordering on child pornography and therefore altered the character to a pre-pubescent for the sake of decency –

which is a double irony in a vampire story! Portions of the novels *The Vampire Lestat* and *The Queen of the Damned* were both used for the 2002 film, *Queen of the Damned*.

Buffy the Vampire Slayer, created in 1997 was a nauseating girly high-school version of Blade and heralded another popular vampire-themed television comedy-drama that was adapted to a long-running hit series of the same name. The series received critical acclaim and usually reached between four and six million viewers of the original airings, according to Matthew J. Wahoske quoting from the Neilsen Ratings. Buffy's success led to hundreds of tie-ins and spin-offs, including novels, comics and video games – not to mention its influence on other teenage-oriented television series.

The spin-off, *Angel*, was introduced in 1999, at the start of *Buffy: Season Four*, and at times performed higher in the Neilsen Ratings than its parent series. The series was much darker since it focussed on Angel – an angst-ridden young vampire who suffered the pangs of guilt and remorse for a century of murder and torture! According to the writer's blurb: "Angel was born in 18th century Ireland; after being turned into a soul-less immortal vampire, he became legendary for his evil acts, until a band of wronged gypsies punished him by restoring his soul, overwhelming him with guilt." Creator Joss Whedon comments that while the central concept behind Buffy was "high school as a horror movie," Angel was a "gritty, urban show" with a more masculine appeal – personally I found the young man tedious but then I am not a 21st-century teenager.

This increase of interest in vampiric plotlines led to the vampire being depicted in films such as *Underworld* (2003) another action/horror film about the secret 600-year-old history of vampires and 'Lycans' (an abbreviated form of lycanthrope); and *Van Helsing* (2004) a tangled tale of Dracula and Frankenstein, which nevertheless grossed over $300 million worldwide; the Russian *Night Watch*, a rather confused supernatural thriller loosely based on the novel of the same name by Sergei Lukyanenko – the first part of a trilogy followed by *Day Watch* and *Twilight Watch;* and the television mini-series remake of Stephen King's, *Salem's Lot,* both from 2004

The *Moonlight* (2007) television series was a paranormal romance concerning a private investigator who had been turned into a vampire by his bride on their wedding-night some 59 years earlier! The *Blood Ties* series (2007) features a character portrayed as Henry Fitzroy, illegitimate son of Henry VIII turned vampire, set in modern-day Toronto; while a 2008 series entitled *True Blood,* gives a Southern take to the vampire theme, being based on *The Southern Vampire Mysteries* series of novels by Charlaine Harris and involving the co-existence of humans and vampires. A sixth season begins in 2013. Another current favourite vampire-related show *The Vampire Diaries,* is a supernatural-fantasy-horror television series based on a book series of the same name by L J Smith; closely rivalled by the fantasy-romance *Twilight Saga,* a series of films also based on the book series of the same name by Stephenie Meyer.

The continuing popularity of the vampire theme has been ascribed to a combination of two factors: the representation of sexuality and the perennial dread of mortality. When reviewing the film element of the vampire genre, however, there needs to be an appreciation of the differences between the screen version and the original novels. Screenwriters are responsible for developing the narrative, writing the screenplay and delivering it in the required format for production, but more often than not only loosely based on the existing novel, which is extremely frustrating for the book lover.

The novel is purchased by the film production company and the screenwriter is then commissioned to turn it into a satis-factory film script. If there is a tremendous love of the book on both sides (as in the case of Peter Jackson's adaptation of *The Lord of the Rings),* then the story is in safe hands, but if the film company is looking for a pure money-spinner based on a novelist's popularity, then there is often disappointment in the finished product.

In all fairness, I can see that there are often valid reasons why characters are merged or omitted altogether, or locations and seasons changed in order to produce a more dramatic effect. Screenwriters have the unenviable job of trying to create a fast-paced film version and cannot afford to indulge in lengthy descriptions or complicated sub-plots that make up a novel. The most frequent complaint is that the ending, and often the central narrative, is altered out of all recognition from the original story (as in *The Hunger*), so to be fully conversant with the vampire genre, I suggest that it is necessary to have read the important novels, both classic and contemporary, and not rely on film and television adaptations for enjoyment.

NB: The films listed here are only a fraction of those that make up the total of vampire themed cinema and television films – many of the others were just too awful to watch!

Chapter Eight

Living Vampires

The Grand Tour introduced the young bloods of England – whose acquaintance I made in large numbers – to crumbling architecture and Gothic ruins and, as a result, on their return they transformed their country estates into "a cross between the *House of Usher* and *Wuthering Heights*, a Heathcliffian blend of artificial mountains, lonely moors and decayed ruins ... the artistic wilderness became the ideal: an atmosphere of gloom and melancholy heightened the sense of remoteness and mystery," observed Donald McCormick in *The Hell-Fire Club* (1958).

I also discovered that a passion for the macabre and the fascination for occultism was as strong as with a similar mind-set of today. To add to the eerie quality of their estates, they planted dead trees and hired 'hermits' to live is specially created caves; even employing men to tame bats, vipers and owls to live in the artificial caves. The 'School of Terror' appeared in literature and there was such a passion for vampires, ghosts, ghouls and werewolves that "some young men insisted on drinking their wine out of skulls especially stolen for them from the graveyards by body-snatchers," wrote Daniel P Mannix in his version of *The Hell-Fire Club* (1970).

The Hell-Fire Clubs were alleged to perform Black Masses and rituals of other occult significance, and were the forerunners of the current role-playing groups that have no serious magical intensions. They were there for the sex, the dressing up and the play-acting – very similar to those '1,215 real vampires' who came out in the summer of 1995 and who claimed to be living the vampire life-style despite the fact that they were still firmly rooted in the land of the *living*! Believe you me, the Hell-Fire

Clubs were a lot more fun.

This 'vampire life-style' phenomenon has also spawned another curious creature – the *psychic* vampire. This extract from *Chance Acquaintances* (1940), reveals that French author, Colette, was fully aware of the cause and effect of encountering psychic vampires, even if she was unaware of the nature of the beast at that time:

> The lessons learned from my instinct, from animals, children, nature and my disquieting fellow human beings. I did not acquire my habitual mistrust of nonentities over a period of years. Instinctively, I have always held them in contempt for clinging like limpets to any chance acquaintance more robust than themselves. We are far too slow in realising that they, though innocent of all personal ill-will, are, in fact, envoys from the nether world, deputised to act as a liaison between ourselves and beings with no other means of approach.

A psychic vampire is a person or being that feeds off the 'energy' of living creatures, although there is no scientific or medical evidence supporting the existence of psychic vampires, or indeed the bodily energy they allegedly drain, according to Benjamin Radford (*Vampires Among Us: From Bats to Psychics*). American author, Albert Bernstein (*Emotional Vampires*) uses the phrase 'emotional vampire' for people with various personality disorders who are often considered to drain emotional energy from others; while Brian J Frost (*The Monster With A Thousand Faces*) writes about a form of sexual vampirism that is said to feed off sexual energy.

Nevertheless those who have fallen prey to psychic vampirism are in no doubt that certain living parties can and do drain the 'life force' from others – intentionally and unintentionally. As esoteric author Melusine Draco explains: "The psychic vampire, can be encountered on several different levels but with a single, main objective being to drain the victim of all energy and ability thus *feeding* in the classical blood-sucking vampire tradition, i.e. draining the life force from a victim. The psychic vampire is doing exactly the same."

Some may ask if these creatures really exist and the answer is 'yes' and they are all around you; and 'no' they are not necessarily enemies – they can be people you know and care about, and who care about you. Think about it. How many times do you meet or visit a friend or relative, and feel tired and/or exhausted while in their company? Or you may find being in their company hard work. This is because these people knowingly, or unknowingly, are draining you of energy. This is only one aspect of a vampire. This 'leeching' of energy can be done by asking continual questions; keeping you talking; demanding your time, or pushing for a meeting. These are all ways of keeping you in their company in order to sap your energy; often they don't even understand what they are doing. They are just drawn to you and need to be in your company as it feeds them and makes them feel better – but they don't know why.

The simplest way to deal with this type of unwitting attack it seems, is to ignore them and keep out of their company; that's the easiest option with this aspect of vampirism and once they are out of the way, the 'victim's' strength will return.

The unconscious vampire is merely a pest and can be dealt with easily providing a concerted effort is made to be unavailable whenever they call upon you for favours or your time. Even telephone calls can be depleting if they go on for long enough, so make yourself unavailable. If it is a family member, ensure that you only see them in the company of other people and make your escape as quickly as you can.

It is fascinating to learn that psychic vampires come in all shapes and sizes and from all walks of life, but apparently it's people with genuine psychic abilities that are the real danger. This type is *consciously* after a victim's physical energy or psychic strength for their own ends. If allowed, a conscious vampire feeds on the weak by posing as being a strong, intelligent leader (i.e. a guru or mentor) whom people are drawn towards – thus ensuring the vampire a continuous feed. Long term, they can become extremely powerful and can have devastating effects upon their victim's health if allowed to continue to siphon off energy. Anyone moving in esoteric circles should always be on their guard and ensure that their protective barriers halt this kind of attention before it can take a permanent hold. Dealing with this type requires more positive action in the form of protective measures and the forthright Ms Draco pulls no punches in her advice:

> More often than not, this kind of psychic vampire will be someone who has professed admiration for your psychic ability and may even be more experienced, or of a higher 'rank'. Don't be fooled! If there is any illness or infirmity that is hampering their own power, they will be after your energy 'like a rat up a drainpipe' as the saying goes. One magical practitioner was highly offended when told by another on whom they had designs, that the only way to deal with a psychic vampire was to destroy it ... the predator took the hint and went off looking for easier prey. Here we would say, 'Trust none!'

Remember the Count's greeting in *Dracula*: "Enter freely and of your own will"? Well, it can only be by an act of Will that the psychic vampire can be repulsed and by making a conscious effort to *never* agree to help or lend something; keep them away from the home front since any acquiescence will scupper any defences that have been put in place. The use of garlic as a deterrent has its roots in ancient Egyptian magical texts so it is a tried and tested formula; bay leaves and hawthorn wood are also effective. Another method that is recommended is crushing garlic flowers or bay leaves in the locks and fastenings of all windows and doors – as a magical protection against psychic invasion – if not against authentic Old World vampires!

As I've already mentioned, the true vampire is a creature of the supernatural and it may seem incongruous to mention what may be viewed as 'magical' techniques, but the world of the vampire often dovetails into the world of the occult; Dracula himself was said to possess incredible occult powers – as do I but on a more modest level. This link to the occult probably stems from the sexual overtones that have long been recognised in the vampire figure and Ornella Volta's *The Vampire* (1965) was an examination of the subject from an erotic viewpoint where the links between blood, sexuality and death were explored in the early days of the embryonic vampire cult. Some things, I've discovered down through the ages, never change.

Living vampires, I was intrigued to learn, are those who have adopted the lifestyle based on the modern perception of vampires in popular film and fiction. David Keyworth, writing in *The Journal of Contemporary Religion* ('The Socio-Religious Beliefs and Nature of the Contemporary Vampire Sub-culture') tells us that within the modern vampire movement, "eroticism has become entwined with the contemporary vampire scene that popular vampire magazines, like *Bloodstone*, include previews of the latest vampire pornography, featuring combined acts of sex and blood-letting." In fact, sexual attraction was the most frequent response in a survey (Joseph D Marco: 'Vampire literature: Something young adults can really sink their teeth into') conducted among a group of college and high school participants, where the participants were asked what they found most appealing about vampires and vampire literature.

There is another element, which I, frankly, would find downright alarming if not blessed with a perverse humour that encourages me to prey on these hapless creatures. Generally these misguided souls do not consider vampirism to be a religion but a spiritual or philosophical path, and there are numerous pseudo-doctrines that are trundled out to explain this strange combined behaviour of sadomasochism, using blood as a fetish or stimulant and psychic/sexual vampirism. Ironically, 'true' vampires look down on the role-players or 'fashion vamps' who like to dress up in period costume, sleep in coffins, and participate in role-plying games such as *Vampire: The Masquerade*, created by Mark Rein-Hagen, etc. Followers of the cult can often be identified by their distinguishing dentistry, having had 'vampire fang dental caps' fitted to give themselves the real vampire look.

Despite the scary appearance, the 'living vampires' tend to be relatively harmless, although many do indulge in consensual blood-drinking – and complain to the police about harassment due to their bizarre appearance! What none of them realise is that no genuine, self-respecting vampire would confer the 'gift of ever-lasting life' onto such creatures. They have already broken one of the most important rules of not drawing attention to one's self, and the reasons why anyone would want to pretend to be un-dead beggars belief – unless they merely wish to frighten the local rodent population and small children.

From a medical standpoint, unlike the above, is the condition known as 'clinical vampirism' or Renfield syndrome – an obsession with drinking blood and named from the character in Stoker's *Dracula*. According to psychology professor Katherine Ramsland (*The Vampire Killers*), it was clinical psychologist Richard Noll who originally coined the expression (1992 – *Vampires, Werewolves and Demons: Twentieth Century Reports in the Psychiatric Literature*), although the term has never gained official recognition by the psychiatric profession as a whole.

Nevertheless, the earliest formal presentation of blood-drinking to appear in psychiatric papers (Archives of General Psychiatry: 'Vampirism – A review with new observations') contributed by Richard L Vanden Bergh and John F. Kelley, who pointed out that sporadic reports of blood-drinking associated with sexual pleasure have appeared in psychiatric papers since at least 1892 with the work of the famous Austrian forensic psychiatrist Richard von Krafft-Ebing. Numerous medical publications concerning the condition can be found in the literature of forensic psychiatry, with the unusual behaviour reported as one of the many aspects of extraordinary violent crimes.

In *The Vampire Killers* by Katherine Ramsland there are a given number of case histories where the murderers have performed seemingly vampiric rituals upon their victims. Serial killers, Peter Kurten, Fritz Haarmann, Diana Semenuha and Richard Trenton Chase were all described as vampires after it was discovered they had drunk the blood of their victims. Clinical vampirism in the context of criminal acts of violence, as well as 'consensual' vampirism as a social ritual, have been extensively documented in the many works of Katherine Ramsland, while others, such as Omas M White, have commented upon the psychiatric implications of 'vampire cults' among adolescents ('Vampirism, vampire cults and the teenagers of today': *International Journal of Adolescent Medicine and Health*).

Dr Ramsland is an author who has published 37 books and over 900 articles, most of which are in the genres of crime, forensic science, and the supernatural. She holds graduate degrees in forensic psychology, clinical psychology and philosophy and written widely on the subject of serial killers, CSI, vampires and ghosts with a special interest in clinical vampirism. The general consensus of opinion appears to be that to be classed as a 'real' vampire one must either be a maladjusted teenager with overactive hormones, or a candidate for a mental institution. I really must consider paying Dr Ramsland a visit in order to alter her perceptions as to whether I am 'real' or not.

There are other poor souls who, due to some medical condition, are inflicted with certain external appearances that cause them to be classed as deviants. As we have seen in an earlier chapter, the wolf, the werewolf and the vampire are often inter-related in folklore and fiction, which brings us to the subject of lycanthropy. This is the professed ability to transform from human into wolf, or manifest wolf-like tendencies, and generally accepted to be the result of magical or supernatural intervention rather than any 'natural' process. Clinical lycanthropy, however, is where someone *believes* themselves to be a wolf (or other animal) and is a mental disorder with psychological causes, as opposed to 'legendary' lycanthropy – which is more akin to shamanic shape-shifting but with homicidal intent.

"Clinical lycanthropy is defined as a rare psychiatric syndrome that has been linked with the altered states of mind that accompany psychosis (the reality-bending mental state that typically involves delusions and hallucinations) with the trans-formation only seemingly to happen in the mind and behaviour of the affected person." A review of medical papers from early 2004, however, ('Lycanthropy-psychopathological and psychody-namical aspects' – P Garlipp, T Godecke-Koch, D E Dietrich, H Haltenhof) lists over thirty published cases of lycanthropy, only the minority of which have wolf or dog themes.

What has been called werewolf syndrome, however, is a rare medical condition that produces an abnormal amount of facial and bodily hair growth, similar in appearance to the mythical werewolf. The medical term is hypertrichosis (also called Ambras syndrome) from the first recorded cases dating back to the late 15th century. The case, referring to Petrus Gonsalvus of the Canary Islands, was documented by Altrovandus in 1642 when he noted that the father, two daughters, a son and a grandchild were all afflicted with hypertrichosis and called them the Ambras family, after Ambras Castle near Innsbruck, where portraits of the family were found. During the next 300 years about 50 cases have been studied with several have been recorded as working as circus sideshow performers in the 19th and early 20th centuries; promoted as freaks having both distinct human and animal traits. The sufferer, however, has no inclination to drink human blood, or howl at the moon.

Porphyria is another medical condition often suggested as having been the cause of accusations of vampirism, due to an over sensitivity to sunlight and producing reddish coloured urine. Informally referred to as the 'vampire disease', this rare condition is genetic and not curable, manifesting the symptoms shown by mythological vampires; the gums are shrunken making the teeth more prominent and canine-life, and they have an adverse reaction to garlic. The term porphyria is derived from the Greek *porphyra*, meaning 'purple pigment' and the name is likely to have been a reference to the purple discolouration of a sufferer's faeces and urine when exposed to the light.

Scientific papers suggested a connection between the disease and vampire belief, but for once common sense prevailed with folklorists and researchers dismissing the idea.

Fortunately for the media, publishing and film industries, the creation of the 'urban vampire myth' gave credence to the belief that the un-dead were alive and well and haunting inner towns and cities, in an age when people are inclined to dismiss such claims as idiotic. Despite this general disbelief in vampires (which makes *my* hunting habits so much easier), occasional reports about them do appear in the popular press, and 'vampire-hunting' societies still exist, although they are generally formed for social reasons, according to Daniel Cohen in the *Encyclopaedia of Monsters*. When rumours spread that a vampire stalked the catacombs of Highgate Cemetery – where I have spent some extremely happy hours before the renovationists ruined it! – in London (1970), amateur vampire hunters flocked to the scene where Sean Manchester claimed (in his dreams) to have "destroyed a whole nest of the creatures." In 2005 there were rumours abroad that a vampire was roaming the streets of Birmingham although local police had received no reports of the attacks and *The Guardian* attributed it to urban legend. And according to an intriguing entry on Wikipedia:

> In 2006, a physics professor at the University of Central Florida wrote a paper arguing that it is mathematically impossible for vampires to exist, based on geometric progression. According to the paper, if the first vampire had appeared on 1 January 1600, and it fed once a month (which is less often than what is depicted in films and folklore), and every victim turned into a vampire, then within two and a half years the entire human population of the time would have become vampires. The paper made no attempt to address the credibility of the assumption that every vampire victim would turn into a vampire.

Which, if we take the good professor's calculations as read, endorses my claim that only those who the vampire chooses will become a vampire in turn; and many of those chosen for blood-letting do not die as a result of one 'attack'?

In Eastern Europe, where vampire folklore originates, the belief in the vampire is now usually consigned to the past, although various communities keep the legend alive for the benefit of the tourists. In small, remote localities, however, vampire superstition is still rampant and sightings or claims of vampire attacks occur frequently, where I often return to put a bit of stick about to ginger up the natives and keep the old legends alive. For example, in Romania in 2004, *The Independent* reported that several relatives of poor old Toma Petre feared that he had become a vampire, and so they dug up his corpse, tore out his heart, burned it, and mixed the ashes with water in order to drink it! Oh foolish mortals.

As I have discovered for myself, vampirism and the vampire lifestyle occasionally manifests as part of modern fringe occultism, with the "mythos of the vampire, his magical qualities, allure, and predatory archetype express a strong symbolism that can be used in ritual, energy work, and magick, and can even be adopted as a spiritual system," according to L Hume and Katherine Mcphillips in *Popular Spiritualities* (2006), although it was not identified as such by David V Barrett (*The New Believers*). "The vampire has been part of occult society in Europe for centuries," according to T H Young (*Dancing on Bela Lugosi's Grave*), "and has spread into the American sub-culture as well for more than a decade, being strongly influenced by and mixed with the neo-gothic aesthetics" – not to mention the BDSM scene and the lunatic fringe.

In his 1931 treatise *On the Nightmare*, Welsh psycho-analyst Ernest Jones recorded his belief that the vampire is symbolic of several unconscious drives and defence mechanisms: emotions such as love, guilt and hate, fuel the idea of the return of the dead from the grave. Which comes extremely close to the suggestion of 'blood-guilt and vengeance' of the ancient world to explain my own manifestation on this earth.

Although more modern and simpler thought is that people identify with immortal vampires because, by so doing, they overcome, or at least temporarily escape from, their fear of dying. "The innate sexuality of bloodsucking can be seen in its intrinsic connection with cannibalism and folklore with incubus-like behaviour. Many legends report various beings draining other fluids from victims, an unconscious association with semen being obvious." Finally Jones noted that when the more normal aspects of sexuality are repressed, regressed forms may be expressed, in particular sadism; he felt that 'oral sadism' is integral in vampiric behaviour – whatever that is.

Nowhere else in folklore and the arts has a creature of fiction had so much psycho-babble written about it than the phenomena of the vampire. When all is said and done, the vampire is generally viewed as an un-dead person that can rise up from the grave (for whatever reason) and wander at will until cock crow, stopping off at a convenient all-night snack bar for a bloody Mary. After a night on the tiles, or clambering up and down the ivy, it retreats to a satin-lined coffin to sleep off the excesses of the night before. From this predictable behaviour pattern, psychiatrists, psychoanalysts, therapists and counsellors have attributed all manner of weird and wonderful diagnosis to the living.

Vampirism also gives an aura of superiority, in that the aristocratic Count Dracula, locked away in his castle alone but for a harem of beautiful women, ventures forth only at night to feed upon the local peasantry. In 21st-century reality, the vampire life style is largely found within the Goth sub-culture, drawing on the cult symbolism of horror films, role-playing games and contemporary fiction to fuel the fantasy – not to mention wishful thinking. And this twilight-fantasy world bears little relation to the traditional vampire, in so far as traditional vampires have been persecuted for centuries and modern 'vamps' are frequently heard complaining that they provoke attack because they contrive to look peculiar.

Having observed all this pseudo-vampirism at close quarters, I think I can be forgiven for questioning the legitimacy of the vampire lifestyle that sucks the blood of its fellow members – for whatever purpose – and consign it to the pockets of other anachronistic social throwbacks that insist on preserving their Teddy Boy, Hell's Angel or Punk image when well past the human age of reason. The things that all these 'eras' have in common is youth's desire to shock the establishment, but none of the other trends based a pseudo-philosophy on something that according to the experts doesn't – and never has – existed.

As much as *you* would like to believe it does!

Chapter Nine

20th Century 'Charnel House' Blues

I've lost count of the number of years I've walked this earth as a vampire, but the most fruitful were those during the 18th and 19th centuries, up to the *belle époque* – that period of twenty years or so before the First World War – that was the culmination of a most delightful and settled way of life – and when everything was seen as a challenge to the intellect. There was still a sense of adventure and discovery in the air, albeit one confined to the few who could afford to pursue the literary or artistic lifestyle *a la* George Byron. This was the time of the Grand Tours, the Hell-Fire Clubs, great art, literature and music, and the *fin de siècle* – the last fling of the 19th century, marked by relaxed morals, taste, customs and decadence. This was, of course, the coming of age of the literary vampire that finally gave us an identity away from grotesque peasant superstition and introduced us to the much wider world.

On the other hand, the most depressing and least exciting has been the 20th century with its increased sexual licence – but without the subtlety and graciousness of the former age. Armchair adventure and reality television means that one never need venture far from the comforts of home to indulge in dreams and fantasy: and was there any period during that century when war and carnage wasn't devastating some part of the world? And if the reality wasn't grotesque enough, there were the ever increasing boundaries being pushed in film and television's 'special effects' world that made the human race immune to the sight of glistening viscera slithering across the screen. The advent of political correctness, however, introduced some extremely strange paradoxes whereby the evening news could show footage of a rebel apparently eating the liver of a dead enemy, while parents were discouraged from posting family photographs on the internet of their four-year old in her bathing suit.

The thirst for sensation continues unabated ... with even teenagers demanding more and more gore in their reading matter but they still want their vampires to have a conscience!

Anne Rice's *Vampire Chronicles* (1976-2003) catapulted vampire fiction out of the shadows of the niche market and into mainstream fiction, with *Interview with the Vampire* (1976), probably the most popular vampire novel ever. Needless to say, there have been critics of Rice's literary style with complaints that Louis remains throughout the novel a petulant figure, self-obsessed and selfish – which he most undoubtedly is! The first person narrative is even more insidious in that giving the vampire a conscience harks back to *Varney the Vampire*, in order that we may develop some sympathy (or empathy) with this cast of the un-dead. Nevertheless, the only true element of horror, with links to classic vampire fiction, is the introduction to The Théâtre des Vampires in Paris where the true decadence of the time still reigns supreme and we can see how the vampires of the Old World looked down on the gauche manners of these visitors from the New World. Even among them, the child-vampire Claudia is viewed as something of a freak, created by someone who did not know, or play by the 'rules'.

The reading public, however, couldn't get enough of this new vampirism with the *Chronicles* selling nearly 100 million copies worldwide; the film version of *Interview With The Vampire* , starring Brad Pitt and Tom Cruise, guaranteed this continued dedication and grossed $36.4 million during the opening weekend. Initially the author was savaged and declined to produce any more supernatural novels, but the second *Chronicle* title – *The Vampire Lestat* had a more positive response and sold 75,000 copies in hardback alone. In creating her characters, Anne Rice still cast her vampires from a privileged background: such as

Lestat de Lioncourt, a French nobleman from the 18th century and Louis de Pointe du Lac, a wealthy plantation owner. Despite this sop to tradition, their behaviour was more akin to monied lager-louts from reality television than the suave and sophisticated vampires of the old school. By contrast, Claudia is from the poor part of town and brings with her the innate cunning and deceitfulness of *her* kind – and, as a result, is much more scary.

These modern vampires differ from the traditional variety and many of their additional attributes are far removed from the folklore of Eastern Europe. The possible 'key' to the popularity of the new generation of 'Rice vampires', however, is the transformation into 'emotional, sensitive, and sensual' beings prone to 'suffering and aesthetic passions', not to mention the supernatural beauty they develop. This may at times appear contradictory and rather incongruous since while some kill to merely stay alive, others play with their victims like a cat with a mouse – and, like Lestat and Claudia, enjoy the 'foreplay'.

The added appeal lies in the vampire's position as an outsider and Rice's books quickly became icons for the Goth and gay communities; a reviewer for *The Boston Globe* suggested that her vampires represented "the walking alienated, those of us who, by choice or not, dwell on the fringe." This viewpoint has had a major impact on later developments within vampire fiction, similar to the feelings Colin Wilson described in *The Outsiders*:

> The Outsider's case against society is very clear. All men and women have these dangerous, unnameable impulses, yet they keep up the pretence, to themselves, to others; their respectability, their philosophy, their religion, are all attempts to gloss over, to make look civilised and rational something that is savage, unorganised, irrational.

Rice bridges the historical time-line and brings the story into the 20th century by having Louis relate his story to a young reporter who quickly becomes mesmerised by the vampire's tale. So enthralled, in fact, that *he* wants to feel those sensations and passions – despite the frank conclusion of despair and loneliness – and begs to be made into a vampire. I must confess in the dim and distant past I experienced these sensations but I learned to channel my energies in different directions and, as a result, even in the depressing 21st century I am a completely fulfilled and self-contained creature.

In marked contrast, *The Vampires of Alfama* (first discovered in a 'remaindered bookshop' in London in the late 1970s), is probably one of those lesser-known treasures of modern pro-vampire fiction. More erotic drama than horror, the story takes place in a fantasy Lisbon towards the middle of the 18th century where Alfama is a "town within the town, sloping down to the waterfront of the Tagus, where it had its own private port. A warren of alleys, terraces and dark passages, where the roof of one house was the cellar of the one above it …" Here is a conclave of magicians, astrologers, alchemists and other outlawed intellectuals keeping out of the clutches of the Inquisition, and into which is introduced Count Kotor and his family.

Count Kotor is a traditional vampire in that he originates from the Carpathians but actively sought out a vampire after discovering "a Chaldean book (translated into Old German by Paracelsus, then transcribed into French, changed and altered), and named the *Book of the Oupyra*." Now a man of immense learning he and his family left the mountains for Prague, the capital city of alchemy, where they lived until the Inquisition renewed its persecution of sorcerers, alchemists, astrologers and they had to move on to pastures new – Lisbon.

The difference with this story is that far from inspiring terror into this closed community, the three vampires are quickly accepted as saviours and healers, and a new vampire-movement is born within the confines of the ghetto. Because of jealousy and revenge the security of Alfama is breached and the community is systematically massacred in their coffins, resulting in the survivors escaping by boat to begin a new life in South America. The chilling finale is magnified with the execution of Laurent, Count Kodor's son; killed by a rival and joined in death by Alexandra who impales herself on the same boar-spear that has pierced her lover's heart.

In *The Vampires of Alfama* , the vampires are not the villains of the piece: in this story they become the persecuted, along with the Freemasons, Rosicrucians and other heresies; echoing the suggestion of the representation of the walking alienated who dwell on the fringe of society. Surprisingly, this novel has never been as popular as the other vampire stories of the time, despite the fact that it had its own distinct stamp of originality in casting the vampires as the good guys. Despite its highly charged sexual elements, opulence and action, there does not appear to be a cinema or television version, and the novel is rarely mentioned in vampire reference works, which suggests that publishers and producers were shying away from the Old World vampire traditions and were only interested in creating something 'new'.

Stephen King's *Salem's Lot* (1975) provided this contemporary approach and has featured in the top ten favourite horror novels ever since it was published. The story revolves around writer, Ben Mears, who returns to his hometown in Maine to discover that the residents are all becoming vampires. Unlike the benevolent Alfama vampires, the Maine variety are more virulent and less discerning about who they 'infect'.

Despite the novels popularity and it being King's own favourite, there is actually nothing original in the good vs. evil scenario, where against all odds Mears and his friend Mark Petrie manage to destroy the 'master' vampire Kurt Barlow leaving the un-dead community leaderless. In order to destroy them, our heroes incinerate half of Maine! The idea apparently came to King while teaching a Fantasy and Science Fiction course, which included *Dracula* in the syllabus, and inspired the thought of what would have happened if the Count had been re-animated in rural 20th century USA.

In his short story collection, *A Century of Great Suspense Stories*, editor Jeffery Deaver noted that King 'single-handedly made popular fiction grow up. While there were many good best-selling writers before him, King, more than anybody since John D MacDonald, brought reality to genre novels. He's often remarked that *Salem's Lot* was *Peyton Place* meets *Dracula*. And so it was. The rich characterization. The careful and caring social eye, the interplay of storylines and character development announced that writers could take worn themes such as vampirism and make them fresh again.

Salem's Lot was first published in 1975, followed by a television mini-series (1979), and *A Return to Salem's* Lot (1987) a film, and in-name-only sequel to the mini-series. A radio drama of the story was broadcast in 1995, and in 2004 a second television mini-series was launched, proving that King's own inimitable writing style has a timeless quality about it, attracting a new generation of vampire-lovers with each fresh media adaptation.

King's master vampire, Kurt Barlow, is ancient and claims he pre-dates the founding of Christianity; possessing the power to 'hibernate' for centuries, and like his predecessor, Dracula, he is highly intelligent and cunning. In the novel, Barlow appears as an ordinary human being, but the 1979 mini-series turned him into a ghastly throw-back of Nosferatu; the second mini-series cast Rutger Hauer as a sophisticated, debonair gentleman, more in the romantic (and more acceptable) mould of M'lords Dracula and Ruthven. If Hauer's brooding presence had been cast in the original cinema version, the outcome might have been completely different.

Now a collector's paperback, Louise Cooper's *Blood Summer* (1976) introduced us to Keith Sharwood, another reluctant, but not quite a vampire. As the review on Amazon observes: "The beginning of Cooper's fascination with tall, gaunt and brooding men is evident in the romanticised depiction of the aesthetic-vampirical Keith …" Again these novels were often panned by literary critics but were generally highly-regarded by aficionados of the vampire genre; writing in the reference volume *Horror Literature: an Historical Survey and Critical Guide to the Best of Horror* (Bowker, 1981), Gary William Crawford says about *Blood Summer*: "This excellent novel concerns Marion and Roland Huws, who, while on a holiday in Cornwall, meets a recluse, Keith Sharwood. Marion's involvement with Keith brings about a widening circle of supernatural horror that leads to 'an insane and bloody murder' and the evocation of a 5,000-year-old Assyrian demon. *In Memory of Sarah Bailey* is the interesting sequel." As Cooper herself describes the novels:

They concerned a character who uncovered an ancient Assyrian curse which turned him into a vampire. He wasn't undead, but he could only exist by drinking human blood. The first book was about how he and the heroine found a way to break this curse. The second told how he was forced to re-invoke it when he came up against a genuine undead vampire. I had vague plans for a series, but nothing ever materialized beyond those two.

The background to the stories is devoid of the familiar vampire-lore apart from a bit of garlic being waved about, and credulity is severely stretched by Marion's casual acceptance of the fact that Sharwood has killed her boyfriend! As another review comments:

Sharwood has a lot of explaining to do, and Marion is surprisingly easy to convince. He admits to being a vampire, except he doesn't sleep in a coffin during the daylight hours and is not repelled by the crucifix. The light of the sun merely weakens and tires him, and he can be killed by any conventional method. Sharwood says: "I'm a human being who can only survive by drinking blood. Human or animal, it doesn't matter ..." Marion resolves to help cure his "vampirism; for actually it's a four-thousand-year-old curse put on his ancestor in Ninevah and passed down through reincarnation ..."

This hovering on the brink of – will he-won't he continue to be a vampire, or can the feisty damsel affect his deliverance in time – has become the signature of contemporary vampire fiction and Cooper was obviously ahead of her time. The plots are a little farfetched as far as the vampire tradition is concerned, but the novels are good fun and have acquired a cult-following over the years. *In Memory of Sarah Bailey* is a Class A horror story and, unusually, a much better read than *Blood Summer*.

Colin Wilson's contribution to the genre came with *The Space Vampires* (1976), a British science fiction horror novel, apparently inspired by the "phenomenon and mythologic legend of psychic vampirism," and the works of horror writer Clark Ashton Smith. It features the remnants of a race of intergalactic vampires who are brought back from outer space and inadvertently let loose on Earth. In a derelict spacecraft, astronauts found the desiccated corpses of several giant bat-like creatures, together with three glass coffins containing three immobilised humanoids, which they brought back for examination. Once back on Earth, the creatures quickly wake from their cyber-sleep and promptly kill their first victim, although these are 'energy vampires', as opposed to the familiar stereotypical blood-sucking variety. They consume the life force by seducing living beings with a deadly kiss, and also have the ability to take control of the willing host bodies of their victims, transferring from one body to another.

The novel's main protagonist is Captain Olof Carlsen, commanding officer of the space exploration vehicle which discovered the vampires' spacecraft, and who discovers that despite their primitive bat-like appearance, they are insubstantial energy-beings from a higher dimension. In 1985, the book was adapted to film as *Lifeforce,* and the novel re-released as a movie tie-in under the different title. The film version differs considerably from the original novel with the vampires becoming a "much deadlier and more prolific contagion in the film" – while the literary variety are inflicted with a human-like conscience and subsequently "destroy themselves upon regaining the ability to see themselves for what they had become." No question of adapt and survive, then?

The ultimate contemporary vampire novel for my money has got to be *The Hunger,* set in fashionable New York. Again the novel searches out the unusual in that it deals with the realistic and *practical* elements of vampirism in the 20th century, such as the methods of attracting their victims and difficulties of disposing of the bodies – a persistent detective is an element that would never have troubled Dracula – and as Miriam Blaylock observes: "The first rule of survival was to take only the unwanted. Otherwise the police just never let go. It was especially foolish to take young children of this era. ... You did your kills in private, and you destroyed all trace of the corpse."

Whitley Strieber's story also differs from tradition by offering an almost science-fictional explanation that these vampires are a different species that bear a physical resemblance to humans, and do not age after reaching maturity. They are extremely strong and difficult to kill, and the fact that they are not actually immortal provides the whole foundation for the narrative. The problems arise when the 'power' transmitted by performing a blood transfusion on a suitable human to prolong youth, begins to wane.

Miriam is a vampire whose life began in the ancient world, and who has created a series of human lovers (both male and females) to provide companionship down through the passage of time. What she doesn't confess when promising they will be together 'for ever and ever' is that while her blood can greatly enhance their life-span, they will eventually begin a rapid and irreversible aging process that cannot be prevented. Eventually they all turn into desiccated, living mummies, encased in heavy-duty caskets to remain by her for eternity. The time frame of the novel covers the disintegration of her current companion and the predatory plan for snaring a new one – the outcome of the novel is completely different from the film version and far more scary. Strieber wrote two sequels to the novel: *The Last Vampire* in 2001 and *Lilith's Dream: A Tale of the Vampire Life* in 2003 following the 1983 film success starring Catherine Deneuve as Miriam Blaylock, David Bowie as her husband, John, and Susan Sarandon as Dr Sarah Roberts.

The vampire genre lay dormant for a decade until the young-adult focussed, *Buffy: The Vampire Slayer*, catapulted the regen-erated vampire onto prime-time television; followed in quick succession by *Angel, The Vampire Dairies* and *Twilight*, not to mention the hundreds of titles in the vampire fiction genre, including comics and graphic novels. This new young-adult (YA) literary revolution that is sweeping the best-selling lists according to Joe Shute, writing in *The Daily Telegraph*, suggests that teenagers weaned on *The Twilight Saga* now want something different from the mainstream: "The rampaging success of the teen vampire saga has led to young adult fiction exploring ever darker avenues." Teen-author C J Skuse also observes that: "I just think it's very important for people to keep getting new and different plot lines so we are not constantly going down the same routes. Love triangles and vampires and all that have now been done so many times before."

Despite this blunt dismissal from a contemporary author, I have to agree with the sentiments of the authors of *In Search of Dracula*, in their belief that the walking dead and the blood-drinking vampire may never entirely disappear. In was only in the 19th century – 1813, to be exact – that England outlawed the practice of driving stakes through the hearts of those who had committed suicide. And although in its native Eastern Europe the threat of the vampirism has been consigned to history and the tourist industry, the lure of the vampire still has its strongest hold in the West. McNally-Florescu also observe that the vampire possesses powers that are similar to those belonging to certain 20th-century comic-book characters. "During the day he is helpless and vulnerable like Bruce Wayne. At night, just as the effete Bruce Wayne becomes the Batman, so the vampire acquires great powers and springs into flight." Let us not overlook the fact that Batman with his sinister caped-crusader image is decidedly psychotic in *his* methods of dealing with the 'bad guys'.

When we study evolution, it quickly becomes obvious which of the world's fauna is at the top of the food chain – those predators whose only enemy is man, with man being the greatest predator of all. Man's only enemy or threat comes from his own kind, or from his worst nightmare: the vampire. As my old mentor John Cuthbert Lawson pointed out – having discovered the 'secret' of his precious *vrykolakas* was to be discovered in the dusty remains of those fascinating Greek tragedies – that our original manifestation was due to obligation of avenging blood-guilt. Unfortunately, those worthy members of the Greek priesthood who learned how to summon up the un-dead in matters of vengeance, having let the genii out of the bottle, lacked the knack of how to get it back in again once the deed was accomplished.

This bodily return might have been 'tacitly expected' in order to directed revenge solely against the author of his (or his family's) dishonour, but it condemned *me* to an eternity of wandering and suffering without reprieve. Do you wonder that I am as I am, having been consigned to the realms of the un-dead at the time when Leonides was defending the pass at

Thermopylae and having survived the collapse of the ancient world, exchanging the tragedies of Aeschylus for the *20th Century Blues* of Noel Coward.

Unlike humans, however, the vampire is not governed by the desire for power or wealth, merely by the need to survive; but unlike a human, the un-dead do not have the option of altering their diet. Bram Stoker credited Count Dracula with a fictional plan for a global population of vampires but echoing the observations of that anonymous professor on Wikipedia, having achieved world domination on *what* would these millions of vampires feed? Whitley Strieber got around the question by having his vampire as a different species, who were "the secret masters of humankind, keeping man as man keeps cattle." Anne Rice saw them as a parallel species with its own social structure of hunter and prey that existed in both the Old and the New Worlds.

In truth, the vampire *must* remain a solitary being in order to survive. To assume responsibility for a companion is to become vulnerable – and I do speak from experience, although I have not indulged myself in creating a female companion for many centuries now. Perhaps this is why I continue to enjoy vampire literature. It brings a sense of kinship without the complications of responsibility for another's safety. I can indulge my passions for the Arts when and wherever I choose, and if this passion stimulates other senses then the perfected hunting instinct can also be described as being an Art in its own right.

When Raymond McNally and Radu Florescu went *In Search of Dracula* they came to a startling conclusion that was laced with a touch of sympathy, if not full understanding:

The vampire's existence is a frightening tragedy, sans goodness or hope, repose or satisfaction. In order to survive, he must drink the blood of the living. And the option of not surviving is closed to him. He should decompose, but he cannot do so. Thus he continues: wanting to live, wanting to die; not truly alive and not really dead. The folklore about him is not based on science, yet it is essentially true. Ten out of ten vampire legends and customs attest what no one doubts; man fears death, and man fears some things even more than death.

Mankind has reason to fear us, since we have conquered what he fears most. And the more we learn to acclimatise, adapt and improvise the longer we will endure.

Epilogue

Although the 'classic' vampire is a relatively modern creation, the image of the handsome and worldly sophisticate has superseded the ancient concept of the blood-sucking demon and, incongruously, now passed into the collective unconsciousness as a 'sex symbol', which of course, makes the hunting of such prey much less of a skill when the quarry is so compliant. As author Douglas Hill observes in *Man, Myth & Magic*, however, to understand the vampire phenomena it is necessary to look behind the curtain drawn over the vampire theme by the moralists of the 19th century.

> In Victorian times explicit accounts of brutality and violence were perfectly proper for wide-spread dissemination, but anything containing more than a hint of sexuality required censorship. This attitude produced the view that vampire legends are just good gory horror stories, grown out of primitive superstitions about the dead. In fact, vampirism is a blatantly sexual motif, riddled with oral eroticism and sado-masochism.

In the good old days, the Eastern European stories didn't shy away from the sexual elements of vampirism, with married vampires clambering out of the grave to "bestow their terrible attentions on their married partners, while those who were unmarried visited attractive young persons of the opposite sex." And it was not solely the blood lust that impelled them – let us recall that in the film version of *Nosferatu*, Ellen uses the knowledge that to defeat a vampire is for a virtuous woman to offer herself to the fiend and keep him in her bed until cock crow. In later tales, both in film and fiction, the sexual angle *was* much more oblique but let's makes no bones about it, the vampire has a very healthy libido and that's what makes the ladies so amenable.

The vampire bites his victims, and as anyone with a rudimentary knowledge of Freud is aware, a bite is viewed a sado-erotic kiss. In *Dracula*, when his harem cluster around Jonathan Harker, they comment that his health and strength mean "kisses for us all" – even the creatures' scarlet lips and luxuriant hair "correspond to widely held folk beliefs about excessively sex-oriented people." Hill also observes that blood is also profoundly involved with sexuality in the human psyche, and modern psychology has shown the predominance of blood and bloodletting in modern erotic fantasies.

Gothic author Maurice Richardson described the vampire legend as a "kind of incestuous, necrophilous, oral-anal-sadistic all-in wrestling match. The vampire embodies repressed sexual wishes and guilts which come from the unconscious world of infantile sexuality." Douglas Hill throws in the comment that this view may unsettle some people who have enjoyed reading fictions like *Dracula*, or Sheridan Le Fanu's story *Carmilla*, with its suggestive lesbian theme. "But it is these undercurrents that are the main reason for the vampire's staying power, in the forefront of our favourite supernatural horrors." All of which is a long way from the concept Jennie Gray suggested: that the Gothic novel "achieved the highest degree of oblique love-making, of steamy twilight passages which walked with consummate art the borderline between suggestiveness and eroticism." Whichever way a vampire's sexuality is viewed from, it's still rather a tall legend for a 2500-year-old vampire to live up to!

Nevertheless, it is also a good idea to shift the blame from the medieval Eastern Europeans and look behind the mind-set of an era that covered the legs of grand pianos and into the very soul of the Victorian death-cult; with the vampires of Bram Stoker and Le Fanu also being influenced by the Irish-Catholic death culture of the time. According to Gothic novelist Stephanie Carroll, there were multiple reasons why the Victorians were obsessed with death, and that was simply because they were surrounded by it. No one could escape from death, even royalty – whose excessive mourning practices quickly became the 'proper etiquette all over the world'. Funerals were elaborate and the more important figures were sent off to rest in massive mausoleums, following heavily attended processions, with glass-sided hearses drawn by black horses.

Highgate Cemetery – with its wealth of Gothic tombs and buildings, particularly the Egyptian Avenue and the Circle of Lebanon (topped by a huge Cedar of Lebanon) feature tombs, vaults and winding paths dug into wooded hillsides – was a fashionable place for Victorian dead. Highgate is often cited as being an inspiration for Bram Stoker, but the only reference to it is in *Bram Stoker's Notes on Dracula: A Facsimile* by Robert Bisang and Elizabeth Miller: "Many people assume that Lucy's tomb is in Highgate Cemetery but we are never told where she is interred."

Footage of Highgate also appears in numerous British horror films and novels, including *Taste the Blood of Dracula* (1970); and the BBC television's *Count Dracula* starring Louis Jourdan (1977). Barbara Hambley's vampire novel *Those Who Hunt the Night* (1989) and released in the UK as *Immortal Blood*, has the main characters visiting the cemetery to examine the remains of a vampire who had taken over an abandoned tomb; not to mention the Highgate Vampire saga that dragged on for years. Incidentally, Barbara Hambley also won the fiction award from the elusive Lord Ruthven Assembly, which recognises deserving works in vampire fiction or scholarship.

Death was part of every-day Victorian life and so it is not surprising that the popular literature of the time reflected that final blasphemy – the defiance of death itself coupled with that other social taboo, sex. It was a ready-made best-selling scenario, which, enhanced with the enduring reputation of England's own blue-blooded Lothario, had Victorian ladies reaching for the smelling salts. There were also echoes in Victorian-Gothic of the Black Death that had had a profound effect on medieval culture, dominating art and literature throughout the generation that experienced it. Le Danse Macabre (or dance of death) was a contemporary allegory, expressed in medieval times as art, drama and the printed word. The theme was always the universality of death, expressing the common wisdom of the time: that no matter one's station in life, the dance of death united all; consisting of the personification of Death leading arrow a row of dancing figures from all walks of life to the grave.

Vampires expanded into popular culture include ballet, film, television, music, opera, theatre, art, literature, comic books and video games. Phillip Burne-Jones's most famous work, *The Vampire*, depicts a woman (believed to have been modelled by Mrs Patrick Campbell) straddling an unconscious man in an image typical of the era in 1897. Rudyard Kipling was inspired by the painting to write his poem *The Vampire* with its refrain ... *A fool there was* ... describing a seduced man – which later became the title of a popular film, *A Fool There Was*, that made Theda Bara a star; the poem being used in its publicity. Theda Bara was nicknamed 'The Vamp' and as a result in early American slang the *femme fatale* was called a 'vamp' – short for vampire – although according to the *Oxford English Dictionary* the term was first used by G K Chesterton and popularised in the American silent film *The Vamp*, starring Enid Bennett. The term inspired many early silent films whose 'vampires' were actually 'vamps' i.e. gold-diggers, rather than supernatural un-dead bloodsuckers. Even in popular music there's the element of the vampire's 'kiss' in the introduction to Meatloaf's *Hot Summer Night*:

> *On a hot summer night would you offer your throat ...*
> *Will he offer me his mouth? ...*
> *Will he offer me his teeth? ...*
> *Will he offer me his jaws? ...*
> *Will he offer me his hunger? ...*

The often unintentional Byronic influence still filters down through the generations of vampiric 'sex idols' and of the original, Colin Wilson observed in *The Misfits:*

> Women begged for introductions, and one of them – Lady Rosebery – was so overwhelmed when she talked to him that her heart began to pound violently and almost robbed her of her voice. Aware of his effect on women, Byron began to make use of what he called his 'underlook', a sudden glance upward from an averted face; it seems to have produced much the same effect as Rudolph Valentino's 'smouldering look' in the 1920s.

Poor old George was an authentic nobleman who lived in a disintegrating abbey and readers of Gothic novels of the period loved 'crumbling castles and mildewed mansions with flapping shutters'. With the publication of *Childe Harold* (1812) he had crystallised the hero the age had been waiting for, continued Wilson. "The heroes of romantic novels were pure and noble-hearted; but people were beginning to grow a little tired of purity – it was the villains who seemed to have all the fun." And these elements of Bryon's personality were mercilessly exploited by both Caroline Lamb and John Polidori when they created Lord Ruthven for *Glenarvon* and *The Vampyre.*

These Byronic trace elements appear in various incarnations through the different generations of literature and film and even more noticeably in the latest manifestation as Angel. He's mean, he's moody but lacks the magnificence of his predecessors; all that angst and introspection would eventually be his downfall because an efficient killing machine cannot afford to have a conscience unless, like *Varney The Vampire*, he *really* wants to die. A vampire can only survive if he is ruthless and calculating, not bouncing around on sofas with *Buffy*-like twenty-somethings.

It's been said – by whom I cannot remember – that the belief in vampires is a poetic, imaginative way of looking at death and at life beyond death. The young of the 21st century, however, feel that they are a long way removed from death. Unlike the lives of people of a plague-ridden, war-torn Europe death has been sanitised in exactly the same way that literary historian Susan Sellers maintained that the vampire has become "such a dominant figure in the horror genre that places the current vampire myth in the comparative safety of nightmare fantasy." In other words, the familiarity of televised and cinema special effects has rendered the *reality* of death and destruction super-fluous ... except for the mawkish, sentimental outpourings when some famous person or local child demands that tons of decaying flowers litter the streets for weeks on end.

The current generation of 'young adults' now consider vampire fiction to be *passé* and demand even more gory narra-tives from YA authors to titillate their jaded teenage palettes. From where I sit and watch yet another fashion come and go, I am prompted to think that like sex, classic vampire literature, is wasted on the young, since this should be considered adult art at its finest. And yet I must confess that these willing young victims are more than eager to offer up their throats to the 'wolf with the red roses'. A fixed stare, the barest hint of a smile across a crowded room and the victim becomes mesmerised like a rabbit 'fixed' by a stoat.

Does it make you uneasy that I walk among you undetected? Have you been lulled into a false sense of security by the welter of vampire lore that dictates what vampires can and cannot do? And what you can do to keep us at bay. I look no different to any other male in the prime of life and could be sitting next to you in a box at the theatre; in the Royal Enclosure at Ascot; or wandering the galleries of the British Museum or the Tate – and yet all the old characteristics are there if you look closely enough, trailing that aura of decadence from a previous era.

So what happens to my victims, I hear you ask? Do they too,

become vampires? The answer is 'no', the majority recover retaining only the faint hint of a memory. Others merely sleep in sylvan settings until the corpse is sufficiently decomposed to eliminate all evidence of the vampire's 'kiss'. Over the years I have perfected the art of changing my appearance at will, and can disappear in a thrice should I inadvertently attract attention. I travel silently and alone – and never by tube since the underground atmosphere I find cloying and disturbing. Unlike my contemporaries, I cast no image in the public mind since Polidori's 'vampyre' remains relatively unknown ... and un-dead!

And yet, in marked contrast to all the other classic vampire stories, it is Lord Ruthven – who is rarely mentioned in the anthologies – who lives to bite another day: *"The guardians hastened to protect Miss Aubrey; but when they arrived, it was too late. Lord Ruthven had disappeared, and Aubrey's sister has glutted the thirst of a VAMPYRE!"* As I've said before, thanks to the penmanship of the Villa Diadoti crowd I remain immortal and eternal but perhaps the final word should go to that anonymous Gothic Society member who remarked: "Once everybody becomes decadent, there is no point anymore."

Sources & Bibliography

The Archetypes and the Collective Unconscious, C G Jung (London)

The Beast Within: A History of the Werewolf, Adam Douglas (Chapman)

Bête du Gévaudan, Abbe Pierre Pourchier and Derek Brockis (Authorhouse)

Concise Encyclopaedia of Heraldry, Guy Cadogan Rothery (Bracken Books)

Countess Dracula, Tony Thorne, (Bloomsbury)

Death, Desire and Loss in Western Culture, Jonathan Dollimore (Taylor & Francis)

Doctors Wear Scarlet, Simon Raven (Panther)

Dracula, Bram Stoker (Penguin)

The Encyclopaedia of Witchcraft & Demonology, Dr Rossell Hope Robbins (Newnes)

Fauna Britannica, Stefan Buczacki (Hamlyn)

The Hammer Story: The Authorised History of Hammer Films, Marcus Hearn and Alan Barnes (Titan Books)

The History of Art, H W Hanson (Reprint Society)

Hollywood Gothic: The Tangled Web of Dracula From Novel to Stage to Screen, David J Skal (Faber & Faber)

Horror Movies: An Illustrated Survey, Carlos Clemens (Panther)

In A Glass Darkly, Joseph Sheridan Le Fanu (Wordsworth)

The Islands of Sorrow, Simon Raven (Winged Lion)

Interview With The Vampire, Anne Rice (Raven)

Isms: Understanding Art, Stephen Little (Herbert)

In Search of Dracula, Raymond T McNally and Radu Florescu (NEL)

Lord Byron, Joanne Richardson (Folio)

Man, Myth & Magic, ed Richard Cavendish (Marshall Cavendish)

The Merciful Women, Frederico Andahazi (Doubleday)

The Misfits, Colin Wilson (Grafton)

Modern Greek Folklore and Ancient Greek Religion, Lawson, John Cuthbert (Cambridge University Press 1910)

The Monster With A Thousand Faces: Guises of the Vampire in Myth and Literature, Brian J Frost (Popular Press)

Myth and Fairy Tale In Contemporary Women's Fiction, Susan Sellers (Macmillan)

The New Believers, David V Barrett (Orion)

The Occult Source Book, Nevill Drury and Gregory Tillett (Routledge)

The Outsider, Colin Wilson (Picador)

Real Cities: Modernity, Space and the Phantasmagorias of City Life, 'Dracula'sFamily Tree' –Steve Pile (Sage Publications)

Salem's Lot, Stephen King (Doubleday)

Space Vampires, Colin Wilson (Random House)

Tales of the Dead, ed by Terry Hale (The Gothic Society)

Transylvanian Superstitions, Madame Emily de Laszowska Gerard (Udolpho)

The Truth About Dogs, Stephen Budiansky (Viking)

Udolpho Magazine, ed by Jennie Grey (The Gothic Society)

The Ultimate Dracula, Hans Corneel de Roos (Moonlake)

The Werewolf Book: The Encyclopaedia of Shapeshifting Beings, Brad Steiger (Farmington)

The Werewolf Delusion, Ian Woodward (Paddington Press)

The Vampire, Montague Summers, (Senate)

The Vampire, Ornella Volta (Tandem)

The Vampire Killers, Katherine Ramsland (Crime Library)

Vampires, Burial and Death: Folklore and Reality, Paul Barber (Yale University Press)

The Vampires of Alfama, Pierre Kast (W H Allen)

The Vampyre and Other Works, Dr John Polidori (The Gothic Society)

Varney the Vampyre, Thomas Preskett Prest (University of Virginia)

6th Books investigates the paranormal, supernatural, explainable or unexplainable. Titles cover everything included within parapsychology: how to, lifestyles, beliefs, myths, theories and memoir.